FOR TH

THE

Shaunta'e

Maria
thank you
Shaunta'e

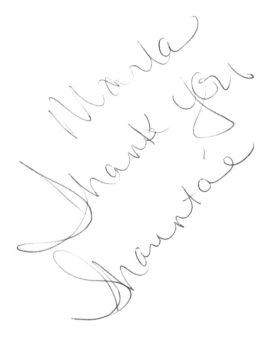

Copyright

For the Love of the Hustle 3

Acknowledgements

Wow this is really Part 3 of the series!!! It was a wonderful year and definitely a learning experience. I met so many great people and awesome readers! This has been nothing but a blessing but I definitely have to give all props and thanks to God for blessing me with a gift and for putting great people in my life. Big ups to my cities HMD and Chi-town who definitely supported book 1 and 2 heavily!!! The love from my cities was off the chain and bigger than I expected. Special, special thanks to my mommy Patricia and to my sisters Nee-Nee and Neitra who heavily got on the grind with me and stayed on the grind with me throughout this whole series.

Thanks to Brittani Williams for killing all three book covers. I surely appreciate it. I want to thank some wonderful people that I met along the way Keys N No Lock Book Club run by Arkeya Keys, Slyce Book Club run by Marilyn Brown (get to know those book clubs), Monique Love, Christopher Ringo, Sassy Ladies Closet, Kosha Jordan, Dion Cheeze, Radiant Readers, Monika Scales-Mitchell, Damion King, Priscilla Murray, Mz.Jetson.com, Nikisha Mock, Kitani Quoweya Jedae Martin, Alexandra Smith, and Shaniqua Morgan. Special thanks to Vanessa Speaks for your wonderful good morning posts. Big huge thanks to Kalena Bowie for being my advance reader. That's just off the top of my head but

I truly thank everyone who supports. I know there are many more!

Be on the look out for L.O.E publishing! Author Tiste about to come with some heat and he's bringing some amazing authors with him, his author Raw pen game is blazing. Shout out to Author Mujahid Akil for rocking with me. Check out his novel "Street Certified."

Big thanks to Gal Capone, Keon Andre, Tree Shelton, Sean Lewis, Fonz Herron, Knox, Tajuana and Jo-Jo for always supporting me without me even having to ask. I appreciate you guys more than you know. To my DJ Cheech Beats for keeping all my events rocking, "Go DJ." I can't wait to the Adult Prom! Everyone who was a part of both book release events I thank you all kindly. Acey, Na-Na, All White Summer, Flawless Perfections, Infamis, Ka'Shay and Supremes Cs thank you! Dawn Banks for always always supporting anything and everything that comes from me! Shout out to Nasty Riders in Indianapolis and Suite 38 for showing me love. I can't forget my cousin Tash for helping me turn up and network in Black Hollywood "ATL." Shouts to DJ Mook and everyone at Blu Cantina for showing love! All events were successes and it is because of all of you! Thanks to my Hustle Bunnies, it's too many of you to name this time but you know who you are. What's understood doesn't really need to be spoken. I love my divas!!!

I had some accomplishments and struggles with this series. Not only did I meet some wonderful people but I also gained some big haters who tried they best to bring ya girl down but still I stand and even stronger. I want to thank you however, because your cackling only made more people curious to pick up the book. Every minute you hated on me another dollar was made. This whole series was about bringing HMD to the forefront and that was accomplished!! Last thing I want to say is just because someone is locked up doesn't mean they don't still need some communication with the world. A letter, phone call, or email means so much! And with that being said I'll end this with Free The Guys!!!!!! My booski Yatta, my uncle Nell, my cuz Keon, my bro Sneaky G, and my homeboy Chuch, if nobody with ya'll I am. I'm out!!!!

SNEAKY

First off I want to thank God for everything.... I want to thank my wife Vickie for going hard and keeping it so real!!I want to thank my sister Tamika aka Boss Lady for going so hard and being bout that life!!! My dude Keon for putting his one two step in motion....I want to thank all the guys in the FEDs who I told about Brand Nu and L.O.E. as well. All my lil homies and real niggas that keep it real as they can under the circumstances......also Team No Lackin! !!! We bout to do it now me, and my two business partners Tiste and Raw!!!! To the whole HMD squad and everybody that supports the hustle and gets down with sp/sneaky-g!! Last but definitely not least, to the boss lady of boss ladies Kitty I luv ya ma!!!

KEON

I'll start off by thanking God who made me and allowed me to live and survive through the circumstances in which I have. To my Cousin/Author Tamika Shaunta'e Howard thanks for being there for me when no one else was and thanks for allowing my story to live through your books. I would also like to thank my very own super Woman my Mother Alicia Thomas for supporting me throughout this whole ordeal. I'd like to give a special shout out to my son for graduating from High school and for staying out the streets. I still think the military is a good place to go but it's your life and you have to make your own choices, just as long as you don't take to the streets and one day become a inmate, convict, which is a modern day slavery. I'd like to give a shout out to the woman who has been there for me, Ms. Lisa Hall. Even though you're not there like you use to be; I still love and appreciate everything you ever did for me. To lady V, Vicky thanks for allowing me to be able to reach out on Facebook. Without you I wouldn't have a voice in the real world.

To my Brothers of the Struggle, first and foremost my big brother and mentor Robert Shipp, AKA Shorty Dope, AKA Amire, you groomed me and taught me how to survive in this abstract crazy world that we live in and not only survive, but to be one of the elite. Styles Taylor, my brother and co-d we fought the death penalty together and were given life plus 50 twice and never batted an eye. We held it down like only real gangsters do. Mike-Mike my real little brother keep doing your thang. Take care of Momma Lisa love yall. Mechiee G my brother from a different mother, even though we don't see eye to eye most times, we still ride for one another whenever it's called for, Bible Inglewood!!!!!!!!!! I have never met someone so disciplined in my life. You have so much that you can teach the world. I pray that the world will one day be blessed with your presence. Pook (Ricky) Kellogg, Big Q, Stop Sign, Big G Ike, G-Man, Big Head D, Hugg, Meat Ball, Boogaloo, Rico, Kirk, Scrappy G, Black Ruben Hughes the burbie King. There are just too many of you good bothers to name, so don't take it personal, stay in the vision.

To my brothers outside the struggle, J-millz, Kerry, St. Louis, Straw, Bone, R-R, BD Gunz, Dollar my favorite Blood NYC will see you again. My CCA niggas doing time behind bars, Bobby Suggs, Shaunta'e Suggs, Pimp T, Will, C-mack, my niggas from the Deuces OB, Radar, KE-KE, and Big Herm. My DC Niggas, yeah you heard me right, Rob, Twin, USA, KEV, and Black.

If I forgot to mention anybody it wasn't personal, just

know that I represent 7-4-14 all day everyday and 027, 424, 026, and 028 to the heart we need to support each other, so buy my cousin's books because she is one of the first to rep our area and tell our stories, saving the best for last, Free Larry Hoover, or let fam out of ADX! If you write me I'll write back

Contact info: Keon Thomas # 06467-027

www.fbop.gov

You Don't Know My Struggle

THE HUSTLE BUNNIES AND SOME OF OUR SUPPORTERS, WE THANK YOU!

FOR THE LOVE OF THE HUSTLE 3

15

Chapter 1 Precious

I'm riding shackled up in a van with Rosa, a Mexican girl I met at Metropolitan Correction Center in Chicago where I was being held while I went to trial for the murder of three D.E.A agents. They set me up on a drug deal for a hundred-thousand x-pills. Two of my girls, Sonya and Neicey saw what was going on and from there it was straight gunplay. When the smoke cleared three agents were dead, along with my girls. Even though I was shot, I lived, and sometimes I wished I hadn't. I didn't get to see Toya, Neicey, or Sonya buried and that hurt me to the core. I couldn't say goodbye so I have no closure.

I actually spent quite some time hooked to a ventilator and handcuffed to a bed. Once they felt I was good enough to be released they took me straight to MCC where I spent a couple years waiting for my trial to start. I had a great lawyer but we still didn't win. They are finally transporting me from MCC to Florida where I will be doing my time. I have three life sentences so yeah I'd rather be dead with my girls. I lost my life to the system at the young age of 16 and even though I had it all, I had nothing to show for it now. The worst part of all this is the fact that I lost Cuz. I love Cuz more than I love myself. Now Shree has him all to herself plus his child off a snake move. I'm supposed to be the one he ended up with. I hate the way my life has turned out. I spent many nights thinking how to end it all. It's funny how you can take someone else's life but too chicken to take your own. I can't stand being locked up. I need to face the facts and stop throwing myself a pity party because even though I'm doing time, I'm treated like royalty or like some type of celebrity. My case was high profile so everyone knew about it; plus enough money on your books will do that for you. Cuz made sure I had plenty on mine.

I got way more things than a person locked up is suppose to have but I'll give it all up if Cuz was able to come visit me. The Bureau of Prisons won't allow ex-cons to be approved on your visiting list unless they're close family like mother, brother, or sister. Cuz isn't any of those technically. Since I've been locked up him and Shree have gotten married for real. That shit tore me up, but he said that he had to do it for a lot of reasons, which he didn't explain. He hurt me something terrible when he told me; still at the same time he's there for me like no other. I never see him except for in pictures that he sends. I'm coming to the realization that my dreams will be my only way of touching him again in life.

I know some people wait until they get locked up to

claim they are crazy in love with their man or girlfriend, but there was never any mistaking the love I have for Cuz and there never will be. I'll admit that my love for him has grown because without him being in my life I don't think I would be able to keep going on. I truly believe him when he tells me that he misses me and Lord knows I miss him as much as a person can possibly miss someone. I'm seriously feeling sick now that I'm being transferred from M.C.C to Tallahassee, Florida. I can't shake the feeling that I may not ever see Cuz in person ever again.

Rosa broke me out of my thoughts and tears. "Baby girl, why you crying?" Rosa and I had become real cool at M.C.C. We were the youngest girls on the floor when we met. Actually we were the only teens on our unit period so we bonded. If anyone knew how I felt and what I was going through, it was Rosa, we had been cellmates for the last year and a half. "I miss Cuz. I was just thinking I'll never see him again." She leaned her head against mine because she was cuffed and chained to her waist like the rest of us in the van. "From what you told me about Cuz, I believe he'll make a way to see you again."

What Rosa said made me feel better. I felt like I had to put all my faith in Cuz. He did promise me that he would get me out at all costs. I still had a chance at appealing so that was some hope. Just as I was beginning to feel better, this ignorant nigga sitting two rows behind us in the van interrupted my thoughts. "Aye shorties! Why don't ya'll lean up or sit up and flash a real nigga some ass or something?" When inmates are being transferred from M.C.C to O'Hare airport male and female prisoners are sometimes on the same bus or van depending on how many inmates are being shipped. That's how we ended up with this bum ass loser who was fucking up my thoughts.

Rosa snapped back at the guy who was trying to get us to give him a show. Under different circumstances I wouldn't mind teasing him, or any other male prisoner, because I know they are missing women just as much as we are missing men. This situation was different though. It had my mind and head in a messed up place. "Fool can't you see that we're chained up just like you? Plus you ain't even worth it even if I wasn't chained up. Now can you leave us alone? Can't you see that my girl is upset?"

"Oh I get it. Ya'll some dikes? That's cool. Hell we all on our way to the joint this might be the last time you'll get to see a real dick." He started laughing really hard like he was about to throw up. He was really getting a kick out of it. He was your normal everyday lame. He reminded me of Ed. I couldn't believe this nigga. He was messing up my already fucked up day. He was pushing me over the edge. Man how I wish I had a gun. I would have loved to shoot his clown ass right in his face. I started day dreaming about how I would kill him and he interrupted that! "Ah you that thot they call Baby girl huh? Yeah that's you! You gotta be the dumbest bitch in the world. All you had to do was give up ya nigga. Now your dumb, stuck up ass is going to the joint, while dude out there fucking with other thots."

This nigga was pissing me off and I swear I was doing my best to ignore him. He just wouldn't shut the fuck up. "You should have told on that nigga. I would have. Ain't no way in hell I'll be going down when somebody else could be doing the time instead." I turned back and looked at him all red eyed with angry tears in my eyes that I wouldn't let drop. If he knew what I was thinking he'd shut the fuck up talking to me.

"Shorty I ain't scared of you or that lame ass nigga you fuck with so save the looking hard shit for somebody else. See I'm going home in six months, and your dumb ass will still be locked up somewhere bumping pussies with some big dike bitch. You know what? Fuck you bitch! I don't want shit from your stupid ass anyway. I'll be home in six months fucking a bitch way better than you, just like your nigga!" I wanted to hurt him so bad because what he was saying was really fucking with me. I just wanted to know his name so I could tell Cuz to please get his ass for me. Rosa saw that his words had me. She bumped into me. "Forget him! Don't pay him any mind. J-Roc is always running his mouth."

"You know him?"

"I just know him from the jail. Girl he one of them niggas that be in the vents talking to them stupid hoes who be into that air vent love affair shit."

"What's his real name?"

"Javon something. He was writing and talking to Jo-Jo on the floor in the end cell."

I turned back around facing J-Roc trying my best to smile and not show my true feelings. "What's your last name?" He answered with a lot of attitude which was making it harder for me to contain myself. "What the fuck you wanna know for?" I was still smiling. "My girl just told me that you were hollering at somebody on our floor. If you're who I think you are I read some of your letters. They were dope. I was feeling you but I don't think you can possibly be the same person who wrote those letters I read."

"Who letters did you read?"

"Never mind, that can't be you. You ain't got that much game." He started smiling and I knew I had him. "Javon Day, I go by J-Roc."

"Sure is, you were writing Jo-Jo. That's my girl. She used to let me read your letters."

"Yeah? So what's up? You gone show me something?"

"Yeah I'm a show you everything. I'm just tired right now. I been up all night, plus I got a headache."

"Man you on some bullshit, just stand up real quick and let me see that fat ass."

"I ain't gone be able to pull my pants down and show you nothing daddy. I'm chained up and my hands are cuffed to my waist."

"I don't care. Yo ass so fat I can see them through the pants."

I stood up and shook my ass back and forth a couple times then dropped it a few times. I could feel my ass muscles jumping. I still had my twerk game down pack. J-Roc and the other dudes got loud and geeked at the little show I was giving. The C.O. yelled, "Hey calm down back there!" Once the C.O's were done checking their guns and loading everybody into the three vans they were ready to transport us to the airport. The three vans pulled out of the basement garage onto Van Buren. This is the time when those of us who hadn't been out in a while sit back and enjoy the sites. I was doing just that. I closed my eyes and let out a big sigh then looked out the window and said goodbye to my birthplace Chicago.

Chapter 2 Precious

I was trying my best to enjoy the view, but the fact was I was tired and hadn't slept since I found out they were transferring me. I dozed off for a little bit. When I woke up we were on the Dan Ryan expressway. "Rosa what are we doing on the Dan Ryan? Aren't we supposed to be going to O'Hare? "I heard them say something about an alternate route. I don't know girl; but girl look at them Hummers right there. They're rolling like Obama in one of them bitches." Sometimes I wondered if Rosa was fully Mexican. She had no accent what so ever.

I looked out the window and saw six big black Hummers pulling up on both sides of the vans. I thought they were the FEDs because the three vans were riding in single file line. There was a Hummer on both sides of each van. I knew they weren't the FEDs when the C.O. on the passenger side picked up the intercom. He began yelling distress codes to someone on the other line. The vans began to pick up speed, trying to out run the Hummers, but the Hummers simultaneously crashed into the vans to stop them. About twenty feet behind us two semi-trucks jackknifed to block off other cars from getting close.

The vans had no choice but to stop. The C.O.'s in our van jumped out with their shot guns nervously yelling, "U.S. Federal Marshals!" Three masked men got out of each of the Hummers with machine guns in their hands pointed at the Marshals. They were wearing bullet proof vests on top of their clothes. It was complete pandemonium. We were chained and cuffed and useless as fuck. We could only sit, watch, and pray we didn't get hurt. The masked men shouted to the guard to throw their guns to the ground. One of the guards in the van in front of us made a sudden move, and two of the masked men gunned him down without hesitation. It was so merciless that the rest of the guards quickly threw their weapons down and threw their hands up. The men in black quickly moved all us prisoners from the vans to the Hummers. They took all the C.O.'s radios, guns, and clothes. Once we were in the Hummers, black pillow cases were put over our heads before they pulled off. The whole incident took less than 5 minutes.

Rosa and I were still shackled together, sitting next to each other. Even though we couldn't see them, we were able to hear them talking, but they were speaking Spanish. I whispered to Rosa, "What are they saying?"
"I think they said something about a warehouse. I'm not that good at Spanish. We didn't talk it much in our home. Now I wish we would have." We stopped somewhere after riding

about ten minutes. We were taken out of the big S.U.V's. and they pulled the bags off our heads and began unchaining us. One of the men began speaking. "There are twelve of you here. You can say that we saved you from the laws of America. There are ten cars with two sets of sweat suits, ten-thousand in cash, and a loaded gun in each car. You don't know us, but trust me we know all of you. You all may leave now! Don't look back, say anything, and remember we know who you are and where you families live. I advise you not to call or go home. Now leave!"

He didn't have to tell me twice, as soon as he said leave Rosa and I took off running to the cars. Before we got into the white Ford Fusion one of the men stopped us and said that we were going with them. Rosa and I looked at each other shocked. We tried to resist. One of the men pointed his gun at us and yelled, "Let's go now! We have no time to waste!" J-Roc had just opened the door to a Chevy Impala. He looked over at us laughing. "Don't pay those dikes no mind. They're in love with each other." I yelled, "Fuck you, you snitching muthafucka!! You lucky I couldn't get a hold of one of them guns because I would kill your ass!"

The men that were dragging Rosa and me to the back of the warehouse stopped struggling with us. One of them said,

"You're a rat? You must die!" They opened fire on J-Roc with their machine guns. I smirked inside watching them solve my problem. Everyone else jumped in the cars and sped out of the warehouse. Meanwhile they led me and Rosa to the back where a white stretch limo was waiting. We were put in the limo with four masked men and pulled off from the warehouse. When we were like four blocks away the warehouse blew up. We were back on the expressway headed towards the airport. I was so confused. *"Who the fuck were these men? Do they want me or Rosa?"*

Chapter 3 Cuz

I've been legit now for a while. I'll admit that I miss the street life, moving bricks and making money, it was a rush. Most of all, I miss having all five of my women at the same time. Since Precious got caught up in that shit with Cocoa and the FEDs the law has been on my ass, watching my every move. I haven't engaged in anything illegal, so they finally pulled off me, but I know they still watching and waiting to hear my name mixed up in anything. I married Shree last month, she's the only one left of my five women who I called the Hustle Bunnies.

Shree and her mother Cheri convinced me in to going to church because I was going through some deep depression. I still blamed myself for the lives of Toya, Sonya, and Neicey; plus for Precious getting locked up. No matter how much money I have I just couldn't bring my girls back or free Precious. The shit was fucking with me mentally. I feel like they gave their lives so I could be rich and live good. Man, I'd give it all up to have them all back in my arms. The square life isn't as bad as I thought it would be and I know it's a safer life for my kids. I have Lil Cuz staying with me from time to time. I love my son no doubt, but for some reason when I look into my daughter's eyes this little lady completely stole my heart. She makes me want to protect her like no other. LaNeice will forever be a daddy's girl.

I may no longer be an active player in the game, but I still get much love and respect from my old crew. They have stepped up and took over the streets. I taught them well. James, Jessie, Ray Ray, and Wayne are all knee deep in the streets getting money. They found a connect and put their money together. Now they're pulling in some serious bread. They each move their own work in different areas throughout Indiana and Illinois. Those guys are nothing to play with. They each got an army of loyal hustlers and killers behind them; with all four of their crews together those niggas can move a nation.

I wish I could get out of this slump I'm in. Since Baby girl was sentenced to all that time, I haven't been able to sleep thru the night. I haven't been in the mood to sexually please my wife either. Shree says she understands, but I don't think she could ever imagine having someone love, look up to you, and be willing to do anything for you to only then end up spending the rest of their life in prison trying to do something special for you. Precious told me she tried to sell all the pills to buy me jewelry worth three-hundred thousand dollars. When I found out that's the reason she did it, it broke my heart. It was

31

my fault that we kept her out the loop. It's was a mistake I'll regret forever.

     I made sure Shree went to visit Precious every visiting day. We were the only family she had. Her mother moved from where they used to live. It's like she vanished. I had Mr. Smith trying to find her mother and little brother but regardless of the outcome I'll always be here. Shree says Precious is depressed knowing she was going to be transported soon. I always reassured her that I would do everything in my power to get her home again. Even if it took my very last penny or it cost me my life, she was coming home. I swear to never give up until she's free again. I didn't have a clue to what my plan was but I was going to think of something.

FOR THE LOVE OF THE HUSTLE 3

Chapter 4 Precious

The four Hispanic guys that were riding in the limo with us weren't talking to us, but they were giving us looks like they hadn't seen women in twenty years. They had me feeling really uncomfortable. We were driven to the back of O'Hare airport where private leer jets were being kept. We were quickly moved from the limo to a really nice leer jet. It looked like the ones they fly in a lot of the videos. The leer had leather seats, a bar, and flat screen TVs. I couldn't help but be hopeful and think, *"Damn Cuz done came up for real."* Then I remembered that Shree told me Cuz was legit now. Whoever they were we hadn't even got to their level yet and we thought we were doing it big.

The guy who seemed to be running things went and sat up front with the pilot. As soon as he was gone the other three men went straight at Rosa trying to take her clothes off. She was doing her best trying to fight them off. She was screaming, kicking, and swinging. I jumped in to help my girl. I know I'm small but I was fucking them up or maybe they weren't fighting back. With all the noise we were making, it brought the head man out the front of the jet. He yelled something in Spanish and the men instantly stopped fighting us. They separated us by seating me three rows ahead of Rosa. When they had us apart the head man smiled and two of the men began to attack Rosa again while the other guy tried to keep me seated. I kicked him in his nuts and he slapped me so hard that it damn near broke my neck. Their leader yelled something again and they stopped their assault on us again. He walked up to the guy that slapped me and hit him in the head with his gun.

Rosa ran and sat with me. She was crying and trying to cover herself up but her t-shirt was so badly torn that her effort was meaningless. I hugged her. "Don't worry. Everything will be okay as soon as I tell Cuz what these muthafuckas did. He'll kill them. We just somehow have to get to a phone." She continued to cry. "I don't think so Baby girl. When he told them to stop, he also told them that there would be plenty of time to rape me later."

"Trust me Rosa. Cuz won't let them touch you, and if they do try something with you I'll fight with you till the end." My mind was spinning. Was this Cuz saving me? Was this revenge for Ricky, or did this have something to do with Rosa? I kept hoping it was Cuz.

The engine on the plane roared louder and the jet sped down the runway and soon lifted up into the air. The jet landed about 12 hours later. I looked out the window and we were landing on an island somewhere. The men rushed us off the plane and put us in jeeps. We drove the bumpy ride on dirt roads in the middle of nowhere for about twenty minutes. The road became smoother and the jungle cleared up. What I saw was like something out of a movie. The scenery was beautiful, it was unreal. This had to be paradise. They took us inside this big beautiful palace. I had never seen anything like this in my life. We were both walking around with our mouths hanging open in awe of this place.

All around the place there were naked females dancing and drinking, or with older men. Some girls were with each other in the most intimate ways. I said to Rosa in a hushed voice, "I don't know where we're at, but I wouldn't mind staying. This has to be better than being locked up for life." She giggled. "Me either. These girls look like their all from different places."

"Yeah I see, but fuck these bitches. I can't wait to see Cuz." I tapped one of them men on the arm. "Hey, when can I see Cuz?" Smiling and laughing at me he said, "Soon, real soon, you'll see all the cousins that you want." I was steaming hot. Why the fuck was he playing with me!

"Hey Baby girl is it?"

"Yeah!"

"Come with me."

"Can my friend come?"

"No, my orders are specific, now come!"

He took me to this very big plush bedroom. There was a patio and the bed was the size of two king sized beds. It was a canopy bed with light colored silk curtains on the sides. "Make yourself comfortable Baby girl." When he left I began rambling through the room. Whoever room this is she had more lingerie then what Neicey and I had in our store. The only type of clothes that were in there were bathing suits, school girl skirts, and evening gowns. I knew Cuz would be coming soon, so I decided to take a bath and put on a sexy outfit. I figured whoever she was wouldn't mind or maybe it was all for me anyway. Why else would they put me in here with these clothes that fit me so well?

I put on this white lace teddy and some cute six inch stiletto heels. I walked back out to where the bed was and stopped dead in my tracks. There was a man standing at the balcony with his shirt off. He looked good and sexy from the back. I knew it was Cuz. My heartbeat dropped to the pit of my stomach and I was filled with joy and tears. I ran to the man praying to God I wasn't seeing things and that it was actually him. He turned around and my heart stopped beating for a few beats. My breathing was stuck in my chest. I couldn't believe it. It was him. It was Cuz. He got me out like he promised. He hugged and kissed me and said in a sexy tone. "You know I missed you Baby girl. I'll never love anyone as much as I love you." Tears just fell from my eyes. I jumped up and wrapped my legs around him. I felt his hardness through his pants. "I know Cuz. I love you too." I came on myself just from kissing him. A loud ass plane flew right over us disturbing my moment. It was too loud.

Cuz walked me over to the bed while my legs were still wrapped around him. I was humping him like a dog in heat. The noise from the plane began to quiet as Cuz was laying me on the bed; but then I heard Rosa calling me right as Cuz was pulling his dick out. "Baby girl! Wake up the plane is here. Baby Girl! They're about to take us out the van!" I woke up feeling lost. I looked around and it dawned on me that I had fallen asleep and dreamt the escape. I didn't even remember falling asleep. Smiling at me, Rosa said, "Girl you were moaning and rubbing on yourself a little bit. You were having a good dream huh?" I was feeling embarrassed because I was so wet. I had cum running down my legs and I was kind of weak. I just smiled to try and cover up how I was really feeling and nodded my head. I really felt like busting out in tears. She must have seen thru my attempt. "Cheer up! This is only the beginning of the fight. Your man won't give up on you. Have faith chica." I smiled and began feeling better because I think she said something like that to me in my dream. Hearing her say it gave me more faith that Cuz would be coming for me one day soon.

Chapter 5 Precious

We flew on the Federal Conair for over 2 hours before landing at the transit center in Oklahoma City. The intake process took like 3 hours. Going through this strip search has become like second nature. I almost know the routine by heart. "Strip, raise up your arms, lift each breast one by one. Open your mouth, lift your tongue, run your fingers through your hair, squat and cough while spreading your pussy. Turn around and spread your ass cheeks, squat and cough again." On top of all that I gotta fill out these dumb ass papers about do I give them permission to go through my mail and monitor my phone calls like I can really say no.

I get depressed when I have to fill out the sheet asking about next of kin and emergency phone numbers. I lost contact with my mama and brother, and through Cuz I found out that my grandma had passed. It eats me up to imagine what she thought of me before she passed. I never got to talk to her either. I list Cuz as my emergency contact and even though I hated to do it, I listed Shree as my second. It always made me sick to my stomach that she had to visit me instead of Cuz. I could tell she hated it as much as I did. I barely talked to her on the visits. I mostly spent my time with Edwina and LaNeice.

40

Although I would miss Cuz, I definitely was happy that I wouldn't have to see Shree anymore.

Rosa and I worked our number and got the C.O. to move us into the same cell as we waited to be transferred to Tallahassee's Women's Prison. Emails from Cuz helped the time pass. He emailed me at least five times a day through Corrlinks. In one of his emails he told me he hired me an appeals lawyer. It made me melt inside to know he was still out there fighting for me to come home. Rosa and I met a white girl named Tammy from ATL. Even though Tammy was white she was built like a stallion standing 5'10' with legs and ass like a video model.

She started hanging with us once she found out we were going to Tallahassee. She was new to the system like us but only had four years for running a high end escort service throughout the county. Rosa asked her, "Why you going to Florida with the type of time you got?" In a deep southern accent she responded. "I slapped an unhappy sister-in-law that happened to work at the federal holding facility in Georgia." She rolled her eyes like the lady she slapped did her way too wrong.

Rosa laughed, but I didn't get it, plus her accent was

super country but it was cute at the same time. She sounded like the white chick in "Beauty Shop." I laughed with them mostly because of how Tammy sounded. "The blue collar bitch had the nerve to step to a diva like me because her sister's husband fell in love with one of my gals and liquidated they bank account." Although Tammy had a banging body, I couldn't picture her being a prostitute. She looked like one of those well off girls from the soap operas. So I asked her, "You were a prostitute?"

"Oh hell naw, me? No way! They claim I was a Madame."

"So you were a female pimp?"

"Oh no darlings. I wasn't anything close to a pimp. Actually I was a make-up artist for magazine photo shoots, music videos, and a few commercials."

I was impressed with all the models and celebrities Tammy knew. She explained to us that she worked with a few black stars but she mostly worked with whites. She told us that she got started because she ended up getting cool with a few models that posed for Playboy and Penthouse. She eventually got invited to high end parties, rubbing elbows with some very rich people. Although they were rich, they were like everybody else. Her first client was the 32 year old heir of the Lexus Empire. He let it be known in a drunken conversation that he'd be willing to pay up to a hundred grand to sleep with Miss

October in the last Playboy calendar.

Lucky for her she knew Miss October and propositioned her with the deal for sixty-thousand. She hooked them up on a date and she kept forty grand and it started from there. In three years Tammy was a millionaire a hundred times over with a black book that could change the lives of the world as we know it.

"I lived a nice a comfortable life off some big names. I like you two. You gals stand out from the rest. You don't seem to have that get over on the next person attitude. I've seen that a lot in the few months I've been in here."

Chapter 6 D.A. Cruiz

"Agent Swanson I can't believe that we can't get anything on Mr. Wilson. We have nothing on wiretaps or the streets?"

"No nothing. It as if he faded out of the streets and none of our drug dealing snitches are willing to mention him.

"We just have to lock-up the right people. I don't know what you guys are doing up there in the Northern district of Indiana but you have a drug dealing mass murderer running around free!"

"Look here Mr. Big Time DA from the Sunshine state, why haven't you been able to get anything on this nigger? If you know he's so got damn dirty, why are you so gun-ho on me bringing him down?"

I didn't answer. I didn't want to tell Agent Swanson that I suspected Cuz of killing Ricky. Ricky was not only paying me off, but he was giving me all the details I needed to bring down dealers to advance my career. He was funding all my political campaigns that would have landed me in the Governor's Mansion in Florida. To say the least I wasn't happy at all about his untimely demise. Waking out of my trance I said, "Look Agent Swanson he ruined the lively hood of some important people."

"That's vague. If it's illegal then take him down for it."

"It's not that simple!"

"Hey don't get touchy or raise your voice at me. You boarder jumpers all seem to get high and mighty because of affirmative action. To me, you're still a bean eating labor worker in my eyes, no matter what position you hold!" He stood up to leave and continued his rant. "Furthermore, me and my office will do all that we can to take that monkey down. You just do your part down here in Indy. He has family down here. Take your own advice and lock up the right people!" He slammed the door as he left.

Chapter 7 Lisa

I sat lost in thought, truly daydreaming in la-la land. It was my grand opening to my 3rd store for Top Notch Wear. My daydream was interrupted by Kim. Kim had been with me since my first store and had become a great friend not to mention my best salesperson. I had made her manager over the new store. "Lisa!" She smiled at me. "I can use a little help. The customers are starting to line up." She looked at me with a confused face. I guess she could tell something was wrong so I quickly answered her in my usual light, sweet voice. "Oh my bad, I'm so sorry Kim. I got up to go help a woman and went to the back to get a pair of red bottoms in a size 8 for the lady. Kim scurried after me. "Boss Lady you alright?"

"Yes, I'm cool." I said with a fake smile.

"Lisa I hope you don't take offense to me saying this, but you've been in a real funky mood lately. Business is going good so what's wrong with you girl?'"

I immediately started to sweat with panic. "What you mean?? I'm cool!"

"Lisa that's just what I'm talking about. It's the way you be looking from time to time. You've been in space lately. Did something happen?"

"What? Nothing happened. You're tripping Kim. I didn't do nothing!!!"

She leaned back and put her hands up. "Okay, damn I didn't say you did anything. I asked if something happened. I'm not accusing you of doing anything but if you need some time I can take over for the day or the week if you need me to. Go relax and when you come back bring back my friend."

"It's that bad huh?" She nodded her head in agreement. "I'm sorry Kim. I didn't mean to raise my voice at you. I can't take any more days off. You have been working too hard to get this grand opening together."

"Working? What work? When you're doing what you love there is no work and you know I loves me some high end shoes. Now go ahead and get yourself in order. Top Notch Wears is in great hands." I gave her a big hug and sighed on her shoulder. "Where would I be without you? I feel like I have nobody else to lean on."

"We'll never know!" I wiped my tears, cleared my throat and said a goodbye to the rest of the staff. I hopped in the car and went home. I made it home about two in the afternoon. Soon as I opened the door I heard loud ass rap music coming from upstairs. *"I know this little nicca ain't home from school."* I thought to myself. As I headed up the stairs just as I thought the music was coming from Lil Rob's room. The closer I got I started smelling weed. I tried to calm myself down before I confronted him. Lately he was being very defiant. He was a teenager who was smelling himself way too much. He was trying his best to imitate his father; well he thought his father was like at his age.

This situation with my son only added to my stress. Not only did he try to act like his dad, he started looking more and more like him. I was pissed the fuck off because he had the nerve to be doing drugs in my house on top of skipping school. Young Jeezy was blaring through the speakers as I prepared to bust in his room. I opened the door and was at a lost for words. Lil Rob had a thick young chick in doggy style position, standing up with a blunt in one hand and slapping her ass with the other. The two didn't even notice that I opened the door. I was mad and embarrassed at the same time. My son was having sex in my house. I slowly closed the door while Lil Rob sang along with the song and slapped the girl on the ass again. "Even if he was, he don't do it like Cuz!"

Chapter 8 Precious

I had been at the transit center for almost two weeks. Even though I had never been to prison before I couldn't wait to get there. The small amount of food and no commissary at the transit center just added to my grief. I began stressing and lost my appetite. All I wanted to do was sleep and dream about how my life was and how I wished I could have done things differently. I started to blame Shree for the death of Neicey and Sonya plus the reason I was in prison. Shree came in and didn't stick to the rules. From day one I knew that bitch was poison. The first night she came home with us she got to sleep with my man alone. If it wasn't for me trying to show her up; I would've never put Sonya and Neicey in danger. I wouldn't be here.

The thought of that night brought tears to my eyes. Shree got to sleep with Cuz without putting in a drop of work but he made me wait and prove my loyalty to him. It dawned on me that maybe Cuz didn't love me as much as he loved Shree. Rosa noticed my down mood and left me alone to be in my thoughts, but then she came running into our cell really excited. "Precious! Get up. I have good news. Your attorney is here. The C.O. just called your name." I just looked at her cause I was still in my thoughts. She shook me. "Bitch get out this bum ass mood and off that bunk. The lawyer your man got you is here!" My heart damn near leaped out my chest. "What?"

"You heard me heiffa. Get yo shit together mamasita and go meet this lawyer so they can get your ass out of here. You want to be with Cuz again right?"

Hearing his name caused me to have mixed feelings. I was just starting to convince myself that maybe he didn't love me as much as he did Shree. Rosa noticed that the excited look on my face quickly faded. "Precious what the fuck is wrong with you? Didn't you hear what I said?" Looking up at Rosa with tears in my eyes I nodded my head. I began sobbing uncontrollably with my hands in my face. My heart was broken and I was confused. "What's wrong?"

"He don't love me."

"Who don't love you, Cuz?" I nodded my head.

"Bitch is you crazy?" Rosa lifted my head and made me look at her. "Let me tell you something. You are one of the very few who has thousands of dollars on your books. Your man got you all type of shit to make sure you were comfortable while at M.C.C, and now you're the only bitch here getting an attorney visit at the transit center. All of this is from the nigga you claim don't love you!"

That put a smile on my face. I got up, washed up, and brushed my teeth. I was feeling better but I still couldn't shake the feeling that Cuz loved Shree more than he loved me. I was escorted to the visiting floor and to a private back room where lawyers met with their clients. When we made it to the room my lawyer was already there. Me and the female officer both had a disapproving look on our face once we saw the old fat man. The fat, black, balding, cheap suit wearing old man wobbled his ass over and introduced his-self. "Hello Ms. Jones. I'm your new appeal attorney Mr. Jefferson." He stuck his fat wrinkled hand out for me to shake. I quickly shook it and let go just as fast.

The C.O. saw I was uncomfortable and smirked as she locked the door. "I'll walk through every fifteen minutes or so. When you're ready to leave pick up the phone and it'll ring my desk." She winked at me and left. I was not thrilled about being locked in this small as room with him. He looked as if he stunk and would hog all the air. He pointed to the chair on the opposite side of him. "Well Ms. Jones how are you doing today?"

"Fine."

"Do you have any questions for me?" He asked as he shuffled papers. "Um yea, can you get me out?" He just stared at me and smiled. I shifted in my chair because he was making me real uncomfortable. "Why you looking at me like that? Can you get me out or what?" He smiled again and removed his glasses and started removing his contacts.

I started to head for the phone for the guard but then I saw he had beautiful dark brown eyes. They were familiar eyes that I knew. I was confused as hell and not understanding what was going on. "Baby girl I'm a do any and everything to get you out." Recognizing the voice but not the face or body had my heart beating at an alarming rate and in a panic. "Cuz is that you? No what the fuck! It can't be!"

"Calm down Baby girl, it's me for real."

Chapter 9 Cuz

"Cuz???" I nodded my head. Tears instantly ran down her face. She almost knocked over the table trying to get to me. "No, no wait. Calm down! We have enough time." I got up and walked to the door to see if the C.O. I paid off stayed on watch. When I saw things were straight I grabbed Precious by her hand pulling out of her seat. She tried to hug me and rest her head on my chest like she use to but the fat suit I was wearing blocked her. "I can't feel your heartbeat Cuz. I need to feel your heartbeat."

"Baby girl you done grew up. Damn!! You fine as hell and done filled out a bit more. Look at that thang you carrying back there." I started spinning her around slowly admiring her whole body. I was looking at a woman now. She started blushing and smiling. She touched my face and tried to pull the mask up but I pushed her back. "Don't do that Baby girl. I wouldn't be able to make it out of here."

"This is weird. It's your voice, your smell, it's you but it's not you. Whatever this is looks real not like a costume." I laughed so hard. "You don't even want to know how I got introduced to this."

"Yes I do. I want to know everything." I began to tell her the story.

Mr. Smith had called me down to his office to let me know he had another great investment for me. He also mentioned on the phone that he had a way for me to see Precious. When I made it to his office I stared out the window of at downtown Chicago waiting on the meeting to start. I was more interested in how he could get me in to see Precious rather than the investment. The phone rang and Mr. Smith answered. "Hello, oh okay send them in."

"You need me to leave?"

"No, you're cool. It's just this couple that's trying to sell me something. You might be interested in it yourself. That's why I called you down." Two minutes later an older black couple walked in. Both looked to weigh close to 300 pounds each. The man spoke up first. "How you doing Mr. Smith? Is this your business partner?"

"Yes this here is Mr. C, and Mr. C this is Mr. and Mrs. Edwards."

I nodded to the obese couple. "Okay Mr. Smith and Mr. C my wife and I have the newest and fastest way to lose weight and we're going to give you the chance to be a part of it first." Mr. Edwards nodded to his wife who shocked the hell out of me by undressing. "Whoa! Hold on mam you ain't got to do that!" What's going on?" Mr. Smith laughed as the woman continued to undress. I was amazed she was a totally different person. Here was this light skinned, pretty ass woman with a nice ass body. "Damn. That was a costume? Mr. Smith you knew about this?"

"Yep. I knew it was something you would be interested in investing in seeing that it would help you see Precious. Not to mention in other activities. Thank you Mr. and Mrs. Edwards can you give us a minute?" They left out the room smiling. They knew they had something great.

"Mr. Smith do you really think it'll work?"

"I don't see why not, just as long as you don't give yourself away."

"If I get caught I'll be the only person in history to go to prison for this." Mr. Smith laughed. "Well Cuz I think that'll be true, but trust me. Have I led you wrong yet?"

"I guess not! How much do they want?"

Chapter 10 Precious

It felt so good to be face to face with the man I love and just listen to his voice and it wasn't over the phone. The face wasn't his but it was him. I leaned over the table and kissed his lips. They felt so good and took me into another world. I was lost and I didn't want to be found. The C.O's keys began jiggling and brought me back to reality. "Daddy, I'm sorry." "Baby girl you have nothing to be sorry for. We all made some mistakes, especially me. I wish I would have told you that Cocoa was working with the police instead of thinking it was best you didn't know." This was new to me. "You knew she was with the police? Why didn't you tell me?"

"Precious I thought you would go ballistic and try to kill the bitch and we already had the FED's on our asses. We didn't need any more heat." I could see the hurt in his eyes. I could tell he regretted holding information back from me. I smiled. "You know me better than I know myself cause ain't no way in hell I could have been around that bitch knowing she was trying to take you away from me. I'm confused though. Why did you allow her to keep coming around us if you knew she was the police?" He let out a big sigh. "Man I thought it was smart to have her around us to show the FED's that we're legit. I was also banking that she would have fell in love with

Neicey." He paused and looked up at the ceiling. "Man I don't know. It was another of many bad decisions I made in life. I fucked up. Now you in here and my girls are never coming back. The shit hurts like hell." The C.O. walked back pass going to her desk.

He gave me that look letting me know the coast was clear. I got up and came around to his side of the table. He stood up and kissed me. He kissed his away from my earlobes and slowly down to my neck. "So what parts of this thing are actually you?" He pulled back and unzipped his pants. "The best parts." He said in the sexiest voice I had ever heard him speak in. Seeing his dick made me cum on myself. I got grip on it and went down on my knees. The passion I felt while giving him head was beyond any sexual act I had ever performed. I was moaning out loud, sucking, kissing, and licking his dick like a starving child sucking a chicken bone.

I must have been doing my thing because it seemed as if he couldn't take anymore of my oral pleasure. He pulled me up, kissed me, and looked deep into my eyes. I kicked off the blue cheap ass shoes, shoved down my pants and panties in one quick motion. Cuz sat me on top of the table, opened my legs, and kissed my pussy. He stuck his tongue insider of me. I screamed out in soft moans. I had never been with him in this way. It was pure delight when he came back up and kissed me. I could taste my own sweet juices. I closed my eyes and savored the moment. "Cuz this is everything I've been dreaming of. The only thing missing is the dick. I got to have it. Please give it to me."

I was eager. I grabbed his dick helping him position it into my pussy. We had a bit of a struggle because of the fat suit but didn't let it stop us. We quickly found a groove. My juices were so hot that he jumped. "Damn you so warm, tight, and wet. I missed you." That made me even hornier. I lifted my shirt, rubbed, and sucked my titties while he was stroking the shit out of me. I was in love and in awe. I was with my first love, my only love, and I didn't want it to end. His pumps got quicker so I knew he was about to come. "No no daddy. I need that! I gotta taste that. Shoot it in my mouth." He pulled out and I swallowed his dick with my lips. I looked him in the eyes and swallowed it all. He moaned out uncontrollably. I sucked him until he got back hard and turned around bent over the table.

He entered me from behind. This time we sexed longer and harder until we climaxed at the same time. We cleaned up with some baby wipes Cuz had stashed in the fat suit. He definitely came prepared. I sat on his lap and we talked until we heard the C.O's keys jiggling, letting us know our visit was almost over. I sat back on my side of the table. "Donald Jefferson is your actually lawyer and he is one of the best appeal lawyers in the country. I promise you that I'm going to do everything in my power to get you up out of here." That made me smile and took all my doubt away. He brought me nothing but joy because I not only believed him but Cuz always did anything he set out to do. "Baby girl you straight in here? Ain't nobody bothering you are they?" I laughed so hard. "Naw, I ain't worried about these bitches."

"I'm serious. Nobody is off limits when it comes to my Baby Girl." I began to look serious. "Daddy you know what? It is this nigga named Javon Day. He's from Chicago somewhere. He's locked up now but I think he gets out in six months. He was fucking with me, calling me stupid for not telling on you." "Ah okay say no more. I'll find out about him and send my nigga Brahead at his body. He knows everyone in the city. Consider it done." The C.O. came and unlocked the door. "Times up." Talking in his disguised voice Cuz said, "Miss

Jones I'm on the case and I'll see what I can do to free you." I couldn't do nothing but smile. "Thank you Mr. Jefferson."

I went straight back to my cell. Rosa and Tammy saw me come back on to the unit. They were sitting and playing cards. I waved at them and went to my bunk. Rosa must have run up to our cell because before I could sit down she was right there. I was rocking the biggest smile she had probably ever seen from me. "Damn bitch the way you were walking to the cell I thought you had to use the bathroom." I just smiled at my friend and she shook her head. "I thought you had an attorney visit, so why you looking like that?" I just hunched my shoulders and kept smiling. "Oh so bitch you can't talk now, should I try to speak my best Spanish?"
"He still loooooooooves meeeeee." I sang out and rapidly kicked my legs out in a running motion while lying on my back in celebration. I told my now most trusted friend about my visit with Cuz.

FOR THE LOVE OF THE HUSTLE 3

63

Chapter 11 Cuz

I was waiting at the Oklahoma airport for my flight back to Chicago when my phone rang. Seeing Lisa's number put a bad taste in my mouth. I couldn't imagine what she wanted cause I didn't too much fuck with her no more but I went ahead and answered. "Yeah?"

"Robert!"

"That's who number you called."

"Um I don't know how to say this." She began crying. "I can't do this Robert. I need help."

"What in the world are you talking about? You can't do what?"

"Lil Rob, live my life, and everything else."

"Man look, stop crying and tell me what's wrong."

She paused for a while and then started talking crazy. "I'm not like you. It's eating my alive. I need to come clean."

"What the fuck are you talking about? Come clean about what?"

"Cocoa dammit! Cocoa!" That caught me off guard. "Cocoa?? What about the bitch? She dead!"

"I fucking know that!!!!!"

"Hey. Hey. Calm down. I don't know what's going on but I'll switch my flight and come straight to Nap to see you."

"Okay but you coming here ain't gone change shit unless you take your grown ass son with you with his disrespectful ass."

"What he do now?" She was on edge. I had never heard Lisa this way. She was really irate. "He brings these little nasty ass girls in my house, fucking like he pay bills, and he bringing drugs in my house!"

"Drugs?"

"Yesss!"

"Look calm down. Like I said I'll be there as soon as I can. Tell him not to make it hard to find him when I get there."

"You need to hurry up before I hurt him."

Chapter 12 Shree

For the last few months I've been spending more time with my mother. I have been spilling my heart out to her. Life with Cuz just wasn't what it once was. It's nothing like I thought it would be once I had him all to myself. Even though Precious is in prison with a life sentence, Cuz still seems to eat, shit, and sleep that little bitch. Now that he's not living the street life he seems to spend more time away from home than when he was in the streets. If I don't initiate sex I believe we wouldn't have any. He did give me the wedding of my dreams but won't make it legally official. He keeps using the excuse that he might legally marry Precious so they can't deny him from going to visit her.

I told my mom all of this and she had the nerves to side with him. "The man is stressed out Shree. I don't agree with the way you all were living in sin, but I can tell by looking in his eyes that he's a loyal man. Shree three young women I mean girls lost their lives getting tangled up in the web of life that he made and he knows it. Then a very young girl who I believe adores him has been sent to prison for the rest of her life. "

"Ma it's like you're helping to make excuses for him when I'm not happy! It's me mommy, your only child and daughter!" Shaking her head at me in disappointment she said, "Shree you're so selfish and spoiled. I'm not making any excuses for that man baby. If you take time off your pity party, you'll see the pain your husband is in. You have a very special man. No matter what he is going through he puts all of that aside to make sure my grand-daughters are happy. They never see his pain or stress. Shree look deep in your man's eyes and you'll see his pain. It's your job as his wife to take as much of that pain away. He takes care of everybody, who's taking care of him? You need to grow up and start acting like a wife and take care of him."

How long was I supposed to deal with him in this slump and pining over a female that was never coming home? I mean I grieved for my cousin and friends but time heals all and he just wasn't allowing any type of healing. I thought church would help but it didn't. I didn't think I was being selfish. I was tired of hearing what if this and what if that! I wanted him to get over it. Life was still moving forward and he was lost in the past. I wanted his full attention. I felt like he was in love with us as package and not individually. I knew damn well I was good enough alone but I'll just listen and take my mama's advice for now.

Chapter 13 Cuz

I pulled up to Lisa's house in a rental car. She was already outside waiting on me. "Come in!" I looked at her to see if I could tell what was bothering her but I couldn't. Her younger son ran out the room and into the kitchen. "Aye stop running in my damn house!" I thought she was being a little extra tough so I tried to soften the mood. "Hey Lil man, what's up?"

"Hey Big Rob!

"What you been up to? Still doing good in school?"

"Yup!!"

"Honor Roll?"

"Un huh"

"Okay then I guess you trying to keep that game chair and get something new."

"Yes Yes I want an I-Phone", he said with the biggest smile. Lisa interrupted, "Boy you ain't getting no damn I-Phone so somebody can steal it. Now go to your room so I can talk to Robert."

Lil Kris put his head down sadly. "Bye Big Rob."

Once we were alone I moved to the same couch she was sitting on. "So what's going on with you?" What's all this talk about Cocoa?" She closed her eyes and blew out air before she answered. "Everything."

"Everything like what?" She paused like she was trying to get her thoughts together. "Well for one your got damn son! He doesn't respect my house or my rules!

"First off, stop yelling at me like I'm your son. Second, like what? What could he possibly be doing that go you this on edge Lisa?"

"Oh man, like I came home early from work and he's smoking weed and having sex with some girl in my house." She paused and there was a moment of silence." "Robert you not gone say anything?"

"I was just letting you vent and get it all out."

"Well I did."

"Okay, look I'll holla at him about smoking weed. Now when he brought the girl home you were supposed to be at work right?"

"And??"

"Come on now! How many times did we fuck in my mama's house? Let's be real about the shit!"

"So I'm supposed to let him fuck in my house because I did dumb shit when I was young?"

"No Lisa, but let's be real! He brought a girl home thinking you weren't here. He wasn't trying to be disrespectful plus I know damn well you didn't have me switch my flight for this shit so what's really going on?"

She began looking nervous. "Robert I can't get over Cocoa."

"Get over what? The bitch been dead for a while now."

She dropped her head and I couldn't believe the next thing that came out her mouth. "I did it! I killed her!" She was crying uncontrollably. I didn't believe her at first but seeing the tears made me wonder. "You killed her?"

Chapter 14 Lisa

I moved my store out of the plaza that Cocoa had her spa in about 3 months after I found out what she did to Cuz. I couldn't believe she snaked me like that. The bitch only got cool with me to take down my baby daddy, who now didn't even want to speak to me. I had finally had him back in my life. The fact that she had fucked up the relationship that we had just started back building really angered me inside. As Precious trial began he grew even more distant. It was already hard for me being as though my husband left me, saying he felt worthless now that Cuz had come back around.

I grew more angry and bitter, feeling guilty like I caused all the mayhem that happened. Cocoa was back in Indianapolis living her life as if she didn't affect my life completely. One Friday I pulled up next to her. "Hey Cocoa, long time no see. What you been up to?" She seemed frightened. "Oh I've been out of town a lot. Lisa I've been meaning to call you. I'm so sorry about everything that happened. I was put in the middle of some messed up shit." "Girl I ain't thinking about that. I didn't know or like them bitches anyway. They had what I wanted. Now it's only one left that I got to deal with. You seen Tiff lately?
"Nope."

"Me either. Hey what you doing tonight? I miss kicking it."
Shocked and surprised that I was being so openly and friendly
with her she said, "I got something I got to take care of at
home."

"Girl put that shit off. I got extra tickets to the Panty Dropping
Concert tonight."

"How the hell did you get tickets to the R Kelly, Usher, and
Chris Brown concert?

"Cause I'm a diva, now Mrs. Thang are you coming with me or
what?"

"Hell yeah!"

"Well we got a couple hours to get ready, but I'm going like
this. We can grab my cousin and hop in the Beamer."

"Okay then I'll run home and change clothes, you want me to
meet ya'll at your place?"

"How about we go pick up Nana, grab the Beamer and leave
from your place?"

"Come on let's roll." I hopped in her car and we pulled off.

I had her drive to Haughville. Cocoa started getting
paranoid. "Your cousin stays over here? It's kind of rough. Hell
I might get carjacked around this area." I laughed, "Girl my
people run shit over here. We ain't got no worries." Pointing to
a rundown looking house, "Pull up over on the side of the
house."

"You sure? This house look abandoned."

"Yeah it's cool let me call her." Digging in my purse I pulled out the .45 that Robert left with me when he went to prison. Holding her hands up her voice shriveled, "Lisa what you doing?"

"What the fuck you think I'm doing? Why you play me like that?" Cocoa was crying but remained quiet. I pushed her in the head with the barrel of the gun. "Fuck that crying shit, tell my why you played me?"

"My man and the FEDs made me do it. We were already cool then they started asking me questions about Cuz. I'm sorry Lisa. I didn't mean for none of this to happen. I wasn't going to go through with it but I know in my gut that Cuz had my husband killed in prison."

"What?"

"Yes he had Derrick killed. That's the only reason I did it."

"One thing I know about Robert is he ain't never killed anybody who didn't deserve it."

"Lisa I'm so sorry. Let's not do this. It's the men that we let in our lives that got us turning against each other. I was wrong but don't let him lead you to doing wrong." I lowered my gun and began crying then raised it back up to her face. She screamed, "I admitted I was wrong. What are you doing? This is not you!"

"You right you were wrong. You were also wrong in thinking that you know me. In all your investigation and plotting you must have forgot I was Cuz's original bitch!" I shot her five times, got out the car, walked through the alley then dumped the gun in the trash can. There was no turning back for me.

■■

Cuz was looking dumb founded as I told him the story. "Lisa is you serious?" Crying I just nodded my head. There was a long moment of silence before we continued. "Okay, wow, um. What's changed since then? Who else have you told this to?"

"Nobody."

"So what changed from then to now that got you stressing?"

"It's always stressed me! I had a nervous breakdown. I just snapped at that point but my mind is coming back to reality. I killed someone."

"Alright look, fuck that bitch! She's dead and she ain't coming back. It's done and over with. You gone kill yourself thinking about it. Make yourself forget about it like it never happened."

"Is that how you do it?"

"Do what?"

"Get over killing people."

"Man you tripping! Quit thinking about the dumb shit. You got two sons to raise and stores to run. Get a new man or even a woman but quit thinking about things you don't need to think about."

It hurt to hear him say get a new man other than him, but we were interrupted before I had a chance to say anything. Lil Rob walked in the house. "What's up Dad?"

Chapter 15 Precious

Me, Rosa, and Tammy finally made it to the penitentiary. I'll admit that I was somewhat nervous about going so far away, but after being in M.C.C the whole trial I was glad at the same time. I at least will be able to get some fresh air everyday. This prison was kind of big. There are 6 building with two units to each building. They put Tammy and me in unit 2A while Rosa was sent to unit 1B. Prison was strange to me. Some of the girls were clicked up by their races while others clicked because of where they were from. In the FEDs you can tell where a person is from by the last three numbers of their inmate numbers. For instance I'm from Northern Indiana so my last three are 027. Rosa's 424, which is Chicago and Tammy's 019 for ATL. There were also girl gangs, clicks, or families, as they called themselves.

We got to the Tallahassee women's prison in the late afternoon and were locked in our cells for count. I was moved into an empty cell so I didn't have a cellie yet. Tammy moved in with a young white girl who was also from Georgia. When count cleared and they called our unit for chow, Tammy and I walked out the unit together to find Rosa waiting on us. We walked to the chow hall together. "Baby girl, who's your cellie?

"I don't have one."

"Damn you seem to catch all the breaks." We started laughing.

"Tammy who's your cellie, or do you have your own cell too?"

"Naw, I have a young gal name Julie from Macon, what about you darling?"

"This Cuban chic named Sofia, she didn't say much."

"We need to move you to our unit so we can be cellies again", I said while thinking how I could make it happen.

When we walked into the crowded chow hall we stood out like kids walking into a liquor store. Being new they put us on green shirts. Once we got our food, Julie stood up and waved us over to sit with her at the table she was at. The table she was sitting at was a real mixed crowd of women. When we sat down she introduced us to everyone. There was a forty something big black woman named Flow who seemed to be the leader of their pack. Flow gave us a run down of all the girls in the mess hall. There were the church girls, the athletes, and the Chicago girls. Other clicks were labeled by their leader's name, like The Flow girls. I wasn't with being known as one of such in such girls, so I already had my mind made up that I was going to see what the Chicago girls were on.

Flow continued, "Now what I'm about to tell you never repeat it. You see the females over there?" She was pointing to a group of Latino chics. "That's Mia. Now her and her girls are into everything bad, but they have access to just about anything you need. Mia and her girls are known for hurting or getting people hurt. If you are trying to do your time and get out of here, try to stay away from them." It seemed like Mia's table were watching us as Flow spoke, then one of her girls got up and headed in our direction. Flow cursed under her breath and the Latino chic walked in our direction, "Shit!"

"Aye Rosa, my home girl wants to see you and your girl right here." She looked at me letting it be known she was talking about me. "Alright Sofie we'll be there." Rosa replied. It clicked at that moment that this was Rosa's cellie. After she walked away Flow explained she didn't want to be in any bullshit as she didn't realize it was Rosa's cellie either. I peeped the old bitch was scared so I reassured her. "Don't worry about it Flow. I appreciate everything you told us and for giving us a place to sit." I looked at Rosa, giving her that look like we might have to fight these bitches when we get over there. "You already know Baby girl, ride to we die."

We stoop up, grabbing our trays, going to see the infamous Mia. To my surprise Tammy stood up also. I looked at her, but before I could say anything she cut me off. "Baby girl! Rosa! We together no matter what, or who it is." Damn

Tammy had some heart. I guess looks are deceiving. When my three woman squad made it to Mia's table, this big man looking bitch got up and cut off our path from standing directing in front of Mia then spoke some shit in Spanish. "Trajeron esta perra blanca con ellos." Tammy was full of surprises because she understood every word. "Excuse me. It's Miss White Bitch." Then Rosa spoke in Spanish. "Cuande nova todos vamos." (When one of us goes we all go).

Mia smiled. "Baby girl I see you have some loyal people with you." I hunched my shoulders because I really wanted to know what this bitch wanted, and then it dawned on me that she called me by my nickname. "Chica sit down its cool. I didn't call them over here for trouble." The whole chow hall was watching us. When Mia stood up all the girls at her table stood, even the ones who weren't done eating. Mia had fourteen girls with her. "Come let's walk around the track."

Chapter 16 D.A. Cruiz

"Hello?"

"Cruiz, this is Agent Miller. We have a hit on the Wilson investigation."

"Where are you?"

"The basement interrogation room three.

"How good of a hit?"

"We have what we believe to be the murder weapon."

"I'm on my way." I can't believe this! I finally got this motherfucker. I was so excited that I began sweating. I knew who I needed to call, the top district attorney in our office, James Cooly. Cooly wasn't currently taking any cases because he was running to be an elected official, but I knew he would love the big headlines that this would get him. If he could convict Cuz of murdering a government witness he would skyrocket is campaign. I quickly dialed his number.

"James?"

"Yes!"

I need you."

"Victor you know I'm not taking anymore cases."

"This one is custom made for you."

"Not interested."

"Hold on! Here me out."

I went into detail and told him about Robert Wilson being suspected of multiple homicides, robberies, and the girls he had kill DEA agents. I explained that we might have him for the murder of a government witness.

"This sounds like it will be great for my career. I may consider this one, but only if your evidence is solid enough for a conviction."

"We're taking off the gloves for this one. Even if we have to free twenty drug dealing punks or murderers, we'll do it. This case is handmade for you."

Chapter 17 Cuz

I've been home a week since my visit with Precious and when Lisa dropped a bombshell on me. I realized that I had been neglecting my wife. Fading from the game and going to a regular life was stressful for me. It's like even though I wanted to leave the game along, the hustle didn't want to let me go. The hustle showed me so much love. I understand that sacrifices have to be made in order to make it to the top, which is what I always wanted but never at the cost of someone I loved. The lost of the most loyal women I've ever had caused me to lose the love for the hustle, but it seems like that bitch is being vindictive and trying me for walking away. I have enough money, a few businesses, and a beautiful family at home. There is no need for the hustle anymore. The hustle game is a cold hearted bitch.

Shree has been running the lingerie store that Precious and Neicey owned as well as her store. On top of taking care of the kids, back and forth visiting Precious for me, she still finds time to take care of our home and be a wife to me. I haven't been much of a husband to her, or man period. I been putting everything else outside of our home above her but this week I'm going to give her my undivided attention.

FOR THE LOVE OF THE HUSTLE 3

Chapter 18 Shree

I made it home a little after seven thirty. Mama had surprised me and picked up the kids and told me don't worry about them for the weekend. When I walked in the house it smelled like a mixture of delicious foods and scented candles. Once I walked through the foyer I notice pink rose pedals on the floor that trailed off into the dining room. Upon opening the glass double doors to the dining room I was completely shocked to find our twenty-four foot dining table gone with Robert sitting on a pile of pillows surrounded by candles with a miniature table in front of him. It looked like a romantic scene out of a Chinese or Japanese movie. Miguel *Simple Things* was coming out of the speakers. I couldn't help but to smile and a tear dropped from my eyes.

I was startled by an Asian woman dressed in a full geisha robe. She gently grabbed my arm and led me to the pile of silk covered pillows across from my man. Three other girls served us an amazing dinner. After we ate he toasted to me with my favorite white wine. "Shree I know I haven't been much of a man to you as of lately, but sweetheart I promise you that things are going to change. This week I'm putting you before everything and everybody. Your mother is going to keep the girls until next week. So you have a whole week to try to put up with me wanting to be with you, on you, and in you."

I licked my lips "Don't make any promises you can't keep."

We kissed then he held up his phone. "I'm cutting this off for a whole week, just to prove to you how serious I am. Baby I love you."

Hearing him say that brought tears to my eyes. "Baby you don't." I was interrupted by his phone. It was ringing *Stunting Like My Daddy.* That meant it was his son calling. He gave me a look like he was seeking my approval for him to answer. He would never expect him to not answer any of the kids' calls so I nodded for him to go ahead and answer it. Lil Rob was so loud and screaming it was like he was on speakerphone. "Dad, they took my momma!"

"What? Who took your momma?"

"The police, they won't let me or my brother near the house. They're asking about you?" I was looking Cuz confused and worried because I myself didn't know what was going on. Cuz continued talking. "Okay listen to me close and do what I tell you. You and your brother meet me at my momma's house."

"What about my momma?"

"I'm a do what I can to get her out, but I need you to take care of your brother for me and get him to grannies'."

"Man I ain't no kid. I got my brother. You just go get my momma. You probably the reason my momma is in jail anyway."

Cuz looked at me and I gave him a raised eyebrow, wondering if his son was right and he was back into some things that I didn't know about. He shook his head. "Look here boy, do what the fuck I just told you to do. You bet not say a muthafuckin word to them people if they try to talk to you.

"Man you just better get my momma."

"I'll see your tough ass in a minute, just leave now. He ended the call and looked at me. "Baby I'm sorry but I got to take care of this. I gotta go!"

"I'm going with you."

"Thanks baby."

"We're together on everything right?" Thinking to myself he did try to do something special for me and that's all that mattered.

FOR THE LOVE OF THE HUSTLE 3

Chapter 19 Precious

When we left the chow hall Mia and I walked ahead of the group. Once we were out of ear shot of the others she continued talking. "Do you like to be called Precious, or Baby girl?"

"It really doesn't matter to me, but Baby girl is good."

"I respect that. Now I bet you're wondering how I know your nickname before you even told me."

Lying, "Not really."

"Oh yea well I'm going to cut to the chase. I was told about you the second the jury found you guilty."

"I don't get it. How and why?" This bitch was pissing me off. Who the fuck was she, and why was she keeping tabs on my case.

"I can see you're getting irritated, but look. We travel in the same circles. I looked at her like she was crazy.

"I have a little sister name Tia, you and your people helped to free her. The name didn't sound familiar to me so I kept staring at her to get to the point. "I'm from Cuba. My family is and has been part of the Cartel but on the legal political side through my weak uncle Felix. Tia was taken from our family and brought to the states by a pervert name Ricky, who you yourself are familiar with." This was the first time that I'd heard the name of the pedophile drug lord being spoken of in a while. Now it was all clicking. Tia must have been the little chic that led us to all his money and drugs after we killed him.

"I remember her! So what you doing locked up in here Mia?" She told me how she snuck to the United States with a group of refugees, some trafficking drugs, and some looking for a better life. She was on a mission to find her sister, so she agreed to bring over ten kilos of coke in order work her way into Ricky's circle. Unknown to her Ricky was killed before she made it to the states. Juan was supposed to meet her and a few others that made it but he never showed up.

"I was freaking out when I found out they were murdered. I thought my sister was dead too. I got dressed and all sexy and went to the club I found out Ricky owned to see if I could find her or anyone else who may know where my sister was. That's when I met Maria." She went on to tell me how Maria told her everything that happened and that her sister had returned home. She offered her a job with her smuggling drugs from Cuba. She was caught after about 3 runs and ended up in federal prison.

I was surprised to hear that Maria had taken over Ricky's business. I kept it as a note to myself to make sure to tell Cuz. She assured me that my time here would be comfortable and thanked me for saving her sister.
■■■

A few weeks had gone pass since we got to Tallahassee. It seemed as though anything I asked for I got it. I requested to have Rosa moved into my cell and it happened the same day. I also got me and my girls our own table in the chow hall. A couple of the Chicago girls joined our table after they saw how Mia respected and looked out for me. There was a chick from the Westside of Chicago named Felicia who was doing 30 years. I was happy to let her join she was cold at hustling. She had the plug on cigarettes and K-2. K-2 was a drug that gives you a weed high but don't show up in your piss test.

Felicia had been getting the sprayed on version of K-2 in by having her people spray it on letters with bogus return addresses. She cut up the letters and sold pieces of it just like it was a bag of weed. The things you think of behind bars are crazy. It's billion dollar ideas in here. I was taking note of everything. "Hey mommy I see you started your own clique with Felicia and them." Mia said interrupting my thoughts. "What's up Mia? How you living?"
"I'm good. I see you got Felicia pushing cigarettes and K-2. I just wanted us to stay with an understanding. You stay with that

and let me run coke and heroin. I need you to communicate that to your crew."

"I'm not trying to step on your toes. I'll let them know."

"If your girls owe they pay, or you pay to stop blood from running. Vice versa if my girls don't pay."

"I wont' have girls with me who use coke or heroin so I'm not worried about them owing you nothing."

Laughing at me, "Then you have some downsizing to do mamasita."

"Like who?

"I'm not going to tell you all that. Baby girl Felicia has been here for awhile and she's a hustler. Keep her close and use her, but don't let her use you."

"If she's such a good hustler why she not on your team?"

"Look at my crew! I don't deal with those outside people."

Then I thought about it. She had all Cuban and Puerto Rican girls on her team. So now she had me thinking if she really fucked with me! She was telling me to watch Felicia but I had made up my mind to watch them both and every other bitch in here!

Chapter 20 Cuz

Shree and I arrived at my mama's house around 9 p.m. My mama was still trying to calm my son down as he paced back and forth fussing and cussing. I was able to hear him cussing as I approached the door. "Damn crackers took my mama to jail for nothing! On life if they don't let her go I'm a kill them bitches. Robert bet not be the reason she locked up either!" I used my key to let myself in catching him off guard. "Or you gone do what?" He looked like a deer caught in headlights. My mama tried to take up for him. "Baby he's just mad and confused right now that's all." She continued rocking his little brother.

Lil Rob had the nerve to play tough with me, by folding his arms across his chest and locking eyes with me. I walked up to him, getting in his face. He only stood about 5'6" and a hundred and fifty pounds. I'm six foot even and weigh two-hundred and five pounds all muscle. "Lil Rob you don't want to do this, now sit ya little frail ass down. That disrespectful shit ain't gone fly in my mama house, you feel me?" He didn't want to back down but I heard him breathing nervously. I raised my voice, "Sit the fuck down!" He sat down on the love seat next to Shree holding his head down. "I know yall mad and hurt behind your mother getting locked up but I'm going to do all that I can to get her back."

Her youngest son stopped crying and seemed to hold on to every word I was saying with hopeful eyes. "But I'm a need all of ya'll to hold it together for Lisa. We her men and if we want her to stay strong, we have to stay strong. Lil Rob now comes the time for you to do your job as a big brother. Play time is over you're Lisa's lil man and it's time to step to the plate. I'm a help you. I got ya'll. I already called a lawyer on my way here."

"Dad when will we be able to go back home?"

"We'll go through there tomorrow. You cool with that?"

"Yeah!"

"Oh yea and for the record if you ever refer to me as Robert again I'm a beat the breaks of you."

Chapter 21 D.A. Cruiz

When Cooly and I made it to the basement where the interview rooms were, we were met by ATF Agent Miller and Indianapolis Homicide Detective Grant who we've worked with many times before. Detective Grant was a partly built, dirty blonde haired 37 year old bitter white man. He dedicated his life to taking down drug dealers. His ex-wife began smoking crack and having sex with her young black dealer. She became addicted to him more than the crack she was smoking. After she got clean she ran back to her young black dealer. To deal with his heartache he devoted himself to his job.

"I think she'll break! We've had her sitting alone in there for over two hours and she's beginning to cry." Detective Grant stated. "Has she asked for a lawyer?
"No."
"Have you asked her if she knows why she's here?"
"It's like she already knows why but that's just an assumption."
"Hmmm, she's either well trained or guilty as hell." Cooly said.
"I told you James, this guy has all his girlfriends trained and they are all killers." I said with an effort to get my point across.
"Victor I'll take it from here. Let me and the two officers handle the interrogation."

"What? Oh no! I'm going in there with you when this black bitch confesses. I want to see when she gives up her boyfriend!" He was looking at me funny. I had forgotten Cooly's wife was black. "Um I didn't mean it like that James. It's just it's a big case. You know what I mean?"

"Yes I do, and like I said we'll take it from here. You can watch from the glass window."

I was pissed. I wanted to be in there but I just stood outside and listened from the glass window as they all walked in to talk to Lisa.

"Hello Lisa. I'm James Cooly a United States District Attorney, and this here is Agent Mike Miller with the ATF, and Detective Jason Grant with the Indianapolis Police Departments homicide division. Do you know why you are here?"

She didn't answer. She just hunched her shoulders. Cooly pulled out a piece of paper from his folder and handed it to her. "Here is a Miranda waiver, can you take a look and read it over or do you want me to read it for you?"

"I'll read it." Lisa said. She read it and then passed it back. "Hold on a second. I need you to sign it to show that you read it." She signed it. "Okay Lisa do you know a woman that most people referred to as Cocoa?" She took a second before she answered. "I want a lawyer."

Chapter 22 Cuz

Shree and I stayed at my mom's house with the kids. My mom had a nice 5 bedroom home in a nice area of Indianapolis. Lil Kris went to the room he always stays in whenever he is visiting to the play the game. The rest of us sat around in the living room waiting for a phone call to find out why Lisa was arrested. I already knew why. It was a little after midnight when the lawyer finally called.

"Robert?"

"Yeah what's up, what they got on her?" I said sound stressed as all hell.

'They have her on potential capital murder." My heart dropped. "Hello?"

"Yeah I'm still here. So she's being charged?"

"They don't have an indictment yet, but this is the government. They'll indict a ham sandwich for impersonating a pork chop."

"How much is her bond?"

"She doesn't have one yet. She'll have a preliminary hearing Monday morning, but I don't see a bond in this case. I'm just being honest."

"So what advice can you give me and my family that'll be best in supporting her?"

"Good question, like I said she has a preliminary hearing Monday morning at 10 am. Show up as a family and quite a few friends to show that she has support. I'll do my best to convince the judge to give her a bond. She owns businesses here and has children so I will definitely argue that."

"How much is this going to cost me?"

"Big, but we'll talk about fees after we see if we can get a bond or not."

"Money is no object."

"This may be a government capital murder case, so money is going to be an object; but with me working the case for you we'll cut most of the expenses.

"What do you think her chances are so far?"

"I haven't seen anything yet, but so far she doing great. She didn't talk to the investigators when they tried to question her. They may have violated her rights already but it's too early to call. I'm on it."

"Thanks Don, this means the world to me. He started laughing.

"That's what you told me about Miss Jones case."

"What can I say? I love a lot, but we can't lose this one."

"We won't lose any of them."

After I hung up the phone my son jumped up. "What's up? When my mama coming home?" It hurt me to see my son so desperate for me to tell him something that I didn't have the answer to. I looked at him trying to find the best way to break it down. I must of took too long because he became irritated. "Tell me!" At that moment I felt like a failure. I knew then that I couldn't protect my family from anything like I always thought I could. "Lil Rob honestly I don't know."

"What you mean you don't know? What she in jail for?" He asked with tear filled eyes. I figured he'd soon find out from the news or a news article so I felt it would be best for me to tell him. "Murder."

He appeared to be stuck for a second, then the tears dried up and he started smiling. "Murder?" Man my mama ain't killed nobody. She'll be home soon. When is her court date?"

"Monday, but it don't work like that. The FEDs got her. They more than likely won't give her a bond." My mother chimed in. "They'll give her a bond. She ain't never been to jail before. Hell she is a business owner and has kids to take care of. Who is she supposed to have killed anyway?" I felt like I had to play on their hopeful vibe. "I don't know, but I'll find out everything that I can. In the mean time I'm going to need you Lil Rob." He looked at me confused so I continued. "To step up, and don't become a problem. You mother needs you now more than ever. Pick your grades back up. Man you were an honor student so let's get back on track."

100

Lil Kris was standing at the edge of the hallway listening to us. Shree held her arms out to him. "Come on in here lil man."

"Lil Kris, this goes for you too. The FEDs will try to use anything they can against her, including you two. Saying things like her kids have bad grades, smoke weed, or stay in trouble. Everything we do from here on out we have to do for Lisa. Can she count on ya'll? Lil Kris smile and said, "Yes. I'm going to be good for mama." Shree bent down and kissed him on his head. She saw how I was looking at my son and grabbed Lil Kris by the hand. "Come on Kris let's go in your room. You can teach me how to play your video game!"

"Well ya'll I'm going to bed. I'll see ya'll in the morning." My mama got up and hugged my son then me and went to her room leaving us alone.

Once we were alone I picked up the keys to my truck and threw them to him. "Let's take a ride." He started the truck up. "Where are we going?"

"Just drive!" We rode around listening to Yo Gotti's new mixtape. Snootie Wild was blasting through the speakers with *Made Me*. I pulled out an ounce of cush and began rolling a blunt. Lil Rob tried to act like he wasn't watching me but I knew he was. I fired it up, hit it a few times then tried to pass it to him. He looked at the blunt then at me, "Are you for real?" I nodded my head. "Man I can't smoke weed with you." I hit again. Talking why holding the smoke in, "Why not?"

"Because you're my dad."

"And don't you ever forget that either. Now take the blunt. You smoke with nothing ass niggas in the streets."

"That's different."

"I'm different." He smiled then took the blunt and hit it. "You bet not tell nobody I let you smoke with me either."

"I won't." Two blunts later we parked back in my mama's drive way.

Chapter 23 Maria

Sitting out on the balcony of my 20 million dollar South Beach mansion, I looked out at the Atlantic Ocean with my partner, lover, and most deadly bodyguard Jackie Martinez. Jackie was a Puerto Rico born Olympic martial artist and a professional knife thrower. She stood 5'5" with thick legs from years of training as a pro athlete and had an ass that caused many of men to lose focus; and often times their lives. Many of people compared her to a thicker meaner version of Eva Menendez. She got up and looked into my green eyes. She could always tell when something was bothering me. "Mamasita what's wrong?"

"I was thinking that Castro's nephew really needs to do away with his communist ways or allow Felix open communication with the U.S. which would give him diplomatic immunity."

"Why worry yourself with things that are out of your control?"

"Because this would change lives, with diplomatic immunity Felix can fly his own plane in and out of the U.S. without Customs or the Coast Guard searching or stopping him. I need to talk to Hector about this."

She started stripping out of her clothes right there as I was ranting. "I love when you think big. You are my Cuban

Queen Pen." She kneeled in front of me and dropped to her knees, parting my legs, and reaching up under my skirt. I rose up a bit allowing Jackie to remove my panties. "But remember the submarines you purchased have been bringing in the coca just fine."

Moaning I continued discussing, "Umm for now, but how long do you think that' going to last, ummmm."

"Long enough! The coca is deep sea diving and so am I, now stop worrying your pretty little blonde head and enjoy this pussy licking."

"Um, damn!" Jackie was making love to me with her tongue.

As I was being orally pleased I thought about how the eight mini subs were only able to bring in fifty kilos a piece twice a week. Thirty-two hundred kilos a month wasn't shit, but I wasn't able to expand or compete with the Mexican Cartel. If only I could get my new friend Princess Aza from Kuwait to use her diplomatic immunity. She could easily stash a thousand kilos on her private airplane at least twice a week. I had met Aza at a private party hosted by Donatella Versace and we hit it off but what she didn't know is that I didn't just own different businesses; I was the Queen of the Cuban Drug Empire.

I had found out that Aza had a deep lust of American Black thugs. The few rappers she had flings with seemed to want to exploit their encounter to the public and the few pretty boy fake thugs I hired to mingle with Aza didn't wet her appetite. I needed a real thug but one that would be loyal to me and smart enough to understand that his relations with the princess had to be kept secret. I had just thought of the perfect man. He was smart, sexy, rough, and real. I began getting wetter thinking about him as Jackie was devouring every drop of my juices. I pictured him naked. I had snuck peeks of him having sex with his girls at my brother's estate.

I wanted him myself but wouldn't let it be known. I began to reach my orgasm thinking about him. I got so into my vision and thoughts that I grabbed Jackie's head and grinded it hard against my pussy with my eyes closed tightly shut. It was to the point where Jackie couldn't lick or suck so she just let me abuse her face as I moaned, "Oh fuck, fuck me you sexy muthafucka. I'm going to cum, yes fuck me." I was thinking back to when Cuz was fucking his girl Sonya with her legs spread wide and pinned over her shoulders. "Yes fuck me!" Pulling Jackie's hair, I screamed out, "Oh Cuz!" I came all over and dry humped Jackie's face before letting her up.

Once she was freed from me, she fell back. "Mimi what's up with that? What's this Cuz shit?" Catching my breath, "Baby I think I just found a way for us to get in and compete with El Cappo."

"Buying bigger subs?"

"No!" Pulling up my clothes and going inside, I started to explain. "We keep the subs we got and we'll get a plane with diplomatic immunity."

"Aza isn't going to let you use her plane.

"She'll let her new boyfriend use it."

"What boyfriend?"

"You'll see."

Chapter 24 Cuz

The White Palace was hosting a Twerk Fest with special guest appearances by Maliha Michel and Roxy Reynolds. 1st Place prize is $5000 plus a professional photo shoot, which will also, earned them a layout for a month in the White Palace sexy event calendar. 2nd place wins $2500 and 3rd place $1000. Twerk Fest was a sold out night with women wearing the sexiest, skimpiest lace, see through outfits imaginable. The fine, the ratchet, big ass to fake ass women came out to play. For an event like this I had to have Sean Dale and Chi Blizz from Power 92.3 host with Raw TV Radio.

I knew money had to be made but my mood was so off. I was there in the flesh but that was about it. Life was throwing me a curve ball. Precious was doing life and my first love and mother of my first child was facing the death penalty or life but I knew the bills had to be paid. Both women needed the best lawyers that money could buy and I had to see to it that neither of them wanted for nothing. Lisa's trial was going to cost millions. I had to hire her two separate experts, psychologist, and a second lawyer.

Lisa had her own money but I had to foot the bill. I knew everything was my fault. It seemed like all hell broke loose because I wanted to exit the game. The night was moving along and women were flirting left and right. I was politely turning them down with a smile. Shree didn't like me coming to the club alone but LaNeice wasn't feeling well. Of course I was fresh to death but simple. I rocked a red Hustle Gang shirt with some Akoo jeans, a fresh pair for J's, a nice watch, and my Cuban link chain with a diamond incrusted HB emblem. I was representing my Hustle Bunnies who would forever live through me.

Thinking about the losses in my life was waking up the beast and hunger in me for blood and destruction. I was losing way too much to the game that I once loved. It filled me with hate. I also hated seeing these new age gangsters take over with no respect for the rules and the law of the land. If it took me to get back into the game to show these new clown ass, tight pants wearing niggas how real gangster get down, move, and live, then it's on. My mind was playing with my heart and the bottle of Ace of Spades that I was taking to the dome was adding fuel to the fire that was burning inside of me.

I was thinking that it shouldn't take much to apply the right pressure on any and all witnesses against Lisa. I'd probably have to kill the officers, detectives, and prosecutor on the case but it could be done. I was squeezing the bottle with murder on my mind when a gentle hand grabbed my arm and took me out of my thoughts. I turned around and saw the beautiful green eyes that I hadn't seen in a while locked with mine.

"Easy killer, you alright?" Forcing a smile, "I am now, what brings you here?"

"Do I need a reason to come visit the best club in the Midwest that just so happens to be owned by a friend of mine?" I was so hypnotized by her beauty, booty, and curves that I temporarily missed the two other sexy women she had with her. The Hispanic one looked like she wasn't happy seeing me holding Maria, and the other was exotically fine, thick, and fat ass. Her nose was kind of big but it could be looked pass. I don't know if it was all the drinking but I was feeling like getting loose with what was standing in front of me. The Arab looking chick was making my dick hard with the way she was looking at me.

We locked eyes and she tried to stare me down until I looked away, which wasn't going to happen. I perfected and won that game with the grimiest gangsters and killers for years so I wasn't going to let a woman beat me at it. The longer I looked at her the more I notice she wasn't that fine but still there was something exotic about her. I wanted her at least for tonight. When the Arabian chic lost the staring battle Maria stepped in. "Oh please excuse me, where are my manners? Cuz this here is my girl Jackie." She cut in grabbing Maria around her waist. "And she too is my girl, okay?" Trying to give me a threatening look, Maria rubbed her hand that rested just below her belly. "And this beautiful lady right here is Aza." Aza began blushing as I reached for her hand which I held on to on purpose. I don't know what's gotten into me because I usually don't flirt; but trying to be the good guy and doing the right thing all the time was getting boring plus I was constantly losing from trying to do right.

Maria waved her hand in front of me. "Excuse me! Remember me?" I let go of Aza's hand. "My bad, I don't know what came over me." I was still looking back at Aza checking to see if she was thick in all the right places. She saw me checking her out and turned to the side, giving me a side view of her ass. Maria tapped me on the chin indicating for me to close my mouth. "We need to talk." Licking my lips looking Aza in her eyes, letting her know I was going to have her, "We all can go to my office."
"Jackie! Why don't you and Aza go back up to the skybox? I need to talk to him alone, don't worry I'll bring him back." She

grabbed on my arm taking me out my zone so that I could lead the way to my office.

"Maria, I just thought about it. How in the hell did you get a skybox? They booked up for the next six months!" "That's nothing. I paid your manager three times the price, and gave the party that was holding it for the night a full expense paid trip to Miami with v.i.p. passes to my club." "I'm impressed." Turning up my bottle I continued. "You did a whole lot so you really must've wanted to see my bad." She got up and walked up to my desk all sexy probably knowing that I always lusted after her. She sat on my desk letting her skirt rise up her thigh as she crossed her legs. "So you're not even going to offer me a drink?" I moved to pour some of my drink into her empty flute. She pulled her glass away and grabbed the bottle. She put the bottle to her lips and tongue and treated the bottle of Ace of Space like a well deserving man's tool.

I never saw her act like this. I'll admit I was loving it. She had my dick hard so I was thinking in other ways. I had to jump back into my right mind frame. I knew thinking with my dick would fuck me up. Yeah she's fine but she's also the silent head of the Cuban Cartel here in the United States. I sat back and pretended to enjoy the show but she saw right through me like I was seeing through her. Putting the bottle down she smiled, "So the slut role isn't working?" I shook my head. We both laughed.

Chapter 25 Cuz

She began to tell me about Aza being a royal princess with diplomatic immunity and her plot of using her plane to get in two-thousand kilos a week. I sat back and looked at this beautiful, evil genius. "And you think that if I fuck her a few times she'll let you use her plane?"

"Nope!"

"So what are you talking about?" She got up off my desk and paced while she talked. "Look Aza has a strong lust for bad boys. Black bad boys, she's a spoiled princess for God's sake. She's been getting her ass kissed by men and women her whole life. She sees thugs as men who will stand up to her. So you know get gangster with her but don't abuse her. Does that make any sense to you?"

"I understand. I still don't see how, if and I do mean if I fuck with her, she'll let you use her plane?"

"Like I was saying if she thought you were the real deal and that you had to go back and forth to Cuba a couple time a week to see your partners she'll do whatever to make that happen."

"I take it she doesn't know who you really are?"

"Of course she doesn't."

"You a trip! You know that right?" She smiled at me. "Let me get this straight. She'll think I'm a King Pin that has connections in Cuba? The bricks are really going to come in with a princess thinking they mine?"

"Right!"

"Are you out of your fucking mind?"

"No I'm not, because you're thinking why would you do this? What would you get out of it? Am I right?" I set back in my leather recliner and nodded at her. "You know a woman named Lisa?"

Hearing Lisa's name come out of her mouth instantly pumped murder back through my veins. She must have seen the look on my face. "Of course you do, well she's being prosecuted by a D.A. named Victor Cruiz. Victor is one of my late brother's associates and I got the same dirt on Victor that my brother did. He just was relocated to Indianapolis. I hear his focus is you. A phone call or two, a couple of packages delivered to him, and he'll make her case go away or his career will crumble as he's locked in federal prison himself."

"What makes you think I can do this?"

"Do you think my brother ever touched me?" I hunched my shoulders. "Well he didn't. I've been plotting to take his operation over for years. Who do you think got Big P to rob and kill my husband?"

"But he cut off your ring finger!" An evil look entered her eyes. "I did that to motivate Big P. I cut off my own finger and told Paul that if he didn't do as I said I would say that he did it."

"Huh?"

"Yea Paul was weak. He missed his shot at killing Juan, so I had to play the kidnapped victim role." This bitch was ill. Who the fuck cuts off their own damn finger?

She came around to my side of the desk and sat in front of me with her legs open, showing me her clean, shaved pussy. "The first time I laid eyes on you, I knew you were the one. I knew you would kill with passion of a real killer. The way your girlfriends rode with and for you; I knew my brother had met his death. She slid off the desk and onto my lap with her skirt up around her waist. As she kissed my neck I whispered in her ear, "What makes you think I'll do this for you? You just outright proved you can't be trusted."

"Because you're loyal and I can free your son's mother."

"I'm married now." She stopped kissing on my neck and looked me in my eyes. "Kill the bullshit Robert. You never filed for a marriage license and this normal life isn't for you Papi. Fucking with the same bitch has to be getting boring to you. I know how you like it."

She knew she had hit a nerve. "You can have Shree, me, Jackie, and Aza, plus Lisa when she comes home. Think about it. With me at your side we'll take the Cartel to new heights. We'll take the coca business over in the states."

"I don't need the stress or money, and I can get the pussy whenever I want it." She was grinding on my hard pipe. "But you need your 1st love back."

"So you're going to blackmail me in order to free my son's mother?" She grabbed me by my face and made us lock eyes. "I'm not talking about her! I see it in your eyes! You have a true love for the hustle!! It's what you were born for." Then she kissed me and reached in my pants to pull my dick out. She eased her already wet pussy over my dick and began to ride me. "Yes, um I've been dreaming about this! Now fuck me!" I grabbed a hold of her ass and pulled her down on me and thrusted upward. "Oh yes, that's it. Fuck me!" She slapped me. "I see you like it rough."

I stood up with her wrapped around me with my manhood still deep inside her. My pants fell to the floor. I bent her over my desk and power drilled her pussy. I was mixed with rage, lust, and hate. I fucked her hard for about twenty minutes before I came inside her. Out of breath laying flat on my desk she asked, "Do we have a deal?" I slapped her on her ass. "Yeah, but we run this shit together. You stay out of my way and if I feel like you're playing me I'll kill you without thinking twice about it." She smiled. "Don't make me cum again. I love it when you talk dirty to me." We washed up then headed back to the skybox section.

Chapter 26 Cuz

Entering the skybox Aza was up dancing looking out the wall size window into the club watching the twerk contest with a drink in her hand. I eased up behind her to dance with her while helping myself to a feel of her round ass. Her silk jet black hair smelled good. She jumped when I first touched her then she continued to dance, but I felt her hesitation. When I openly smelled her neck, she pulled back, looking mean with an attitude. "I didn't say you could do all that!" Then she moved my hands from her lovely behind and walked over to the bar. I joined Aza at the bar continuing my pursuit. The bartender Tonda was closely observing our cat and mouse chase. She raised her eyebrow and gave me a confused look. It was probably because she had never seen me pursue a woman, or maybe it was because I kept turning her away.

"Where you from?"
"Kuwait, and I'm sure Maria told you that already." She turned and tried to give Maria the evil eye. Maria smiled and hunched her shoulders. "Naw she didn't tell me much of anything about you." She looked at me up and down, "Oh I'm sure she told you plenty or paid you." Looking offended I said, "Paid me? What the fuck you talking about?"

"Come on now Cuz is it? Yea I'm sure she paid you. I mean look at you, you're exactly my type and you almost seem real." Then she reached out and felt my arm. I snatched away from her then pulled her close and whispered in her ear. "Look her lil mama, I don't know what's going on between you and Maria, but nobody pays me off like some trick ass nigga. Bitch it don't get no realer than me." I pushed away from her. "Tonda take this soft ass Ace of Spades and give me a double shot of Henn." Tonda smiled and filled my order and smirked at Aza. Aza was standing there looking stuck like she was star struck or something.

Chapter 27 Maria

I saw the change in Cuz's attitude and joined them at the bar. "Trouble in paradise?"

"Shorty, you and your girl got a nigga fucked up for real." He hit his drink. "She talking about a nigga being paid and I seem real." I couldn't do anything but look surprised. I wasn't aware that Aza was hip to my little games. "I'm so sorry Cuz." I grabbed Aza by her arm and led her to the other side of the room. When we were seated on the leather sectional I pleaded my case to her. "Aza I didn't pay him. I'll admit that I did in the past because I didn't think you were ready for a real thug but he's the real thing. He owns this club and he's a drug dealer, a real drug dealer, he's not local. He's stressed right now but usually he's not so hostile." She looked as if she wasn't buying it so I baited her more. "You know how rich men in your country have more than one wife?" She nodded her head. "Well he had six wives. He lost 3 to death in this life he lives and two are currently locked up facing life sentences. He only has one alive and doing well."

Aza was looking at Cuz like she truly admired him. "You didn't tell him I was a princess?"

"Yes I'm sorry." She starting smiling, "And he still called me a bitch?" I nodded. "How can I get back into his good graces Maria?"

"By the way he was looking at your ass, nothing." We both laughed. "Call him over here."

"Nope let's go to him."

Chapter 28 Cuz

When I woke up naked on the floor of my office with three naked women on me; it made me feel like I had my girls back for a minute. I haven't had a mind blowing foursome in a while. I didn't even know that Maria was into women, and Aza man was she a screamer. The way she yelled and moaned stroked my ego back to new heights. This is the way I'm supposed to be living. Maybe Maria was right. I couldn't help but smile as I admired the naked beauty that surrounded me. Aza was wrapped up under me just the way Precious used to. Maria was on my left and Jackie was behind her.

Everyone was still asleep except for Jackie. She was giving me the evil eye, which made me remember that she wouldn't come close to my dick or close to Aza. This bitch was solely about Maria. I began smiling harder when I remembered how she was looking when I was fucking Maria from the back. Our mean mugging event was interrupted when I heard the faint sound of a buzzing phone. I slowly reached over Aza and grabbed my phone. I had 60 missed calls. 57 were from Shree and 3 unknown. This was the first time in a long time I've stayed out like this. For the first time in a long time I didn't know what I was doing or how I was going to deal with the situation.

When I put my phone down I noticed a pair of beautiful hazel eyes watching me. This woman was going to shake my world up as I knew it. "One of your wives?" Aza surprised me with the question and she must have seen it on my face. "Maria told me you had wives."

"She did?" Aza nodded her pretty head. "What else did she tell you?" She hunched her shoulders. "Enough to make me want you." She grabbed my morning, well afternoon erection. "I see you're ready to go at it again."

"Shorty I stay ready." She continued to stroke me. "I hate to stop you, but I have a million things to tend to. I can't afford to lay up all day, but trust me if you are willing we will have plenty of time for this and much more. I'm not the stepping out kind of man, it 's just that you're." I paused because I was lost for words. I was attaching to her quickly. It was something about her like Precious that told me she'd be loyal. "I don't know. It's just something about you I can't resist."

She smiled, still hold on to my dick, she kissed me. "You're resisting me now!" I laughed. "I'm making myself do it." Then I stood up, waking up Maria. Standing naked with my hard dick at full attention, Maria sat up and smiled. Looking at my dick she said, "Well good morning to you too!" I looked down at myself. "Very funny; ladies I really enjoyed myself all night last night. I'm a busy man and I have things that I have to take care of and get right." I finished getting dressed.

Maria kissed Jackie and Jackie started caressing her breast. "Aza this is the first time we've been sexual with each other and he wants to run out on us?" Aza agreed. "I can't imagine what's so important that an aroused man would be willing to walk out on us like this!"
"Aza our friend Robert better known as Cuz is a major business man." She closed her eyes enjoying the treatment that Jackie was giving her. She stopped Jackie from going down on her and gave me a very serious look. "Aza I know how to not only get Cuz's attention, but keep it." Lying next to Maria while Maria rubbed her thigh Aza moaned out, "How?"
"Cuz Aza has her own private plane and she has diplomatic immunity. She can fly you privately to Cuba for your meetings with my family undisturbed."

Now she was smoothly rubbing her fingers through Aza's clean shaven pussy making her wet. "Isn't that right Aza?" Sucking her bottom lip, cuffing her own breast, Aza locked eyes with me and spread her legs wide open and moaned out, "Anything for you Robert." She closed her eyes as

Maria inserted a well manicured finger in her hot pussy. Maria gave me a demanding look. I couldn't help but to think, *"This bitch is truly conniving!"* Then she continued. "We don't mind sharing you with Lisa and the others." I guess that was my queue. I took my pants back off. My phone hummed as Shree was calling again. I turned my phone off.

■ ■

After that episode at my club I've been with Maria, Aza, and Jackie damn near everyday. Aza knew about my other girls and she didn't understand why Shree didn't want to be nice to her or accept her. When I told Shree about the situation she went ballistic. "I'm not living like that again!"

"Listen baby! I have to do this! This will get Lisa off on that murder charge!"

"Bullshit! That snake ass Cuban drug dealing bitch has been after you from day one! The first time I met that bitch I knew she wanted you. Now your dumb ass is going to let her trick you into thinking she can't get Lisa out of jail if you be with her?"

"It's not just her."

"Oh how can I forget! You have to be with the Arab bitch too!"

"She's not Arabian, she's from Kuwait!"

"Get out!"

"What??"

"You heard me, get the fuck out!

127

"You got the game fucked up! This is my shit. This is how I get down. This is how your ass met me, now you want to come in here trying to change some shit? How many women did I have when you came begging to get down?"

She started crying hysterically. "You promised me! You promised me that things would be different. That you were going to change for Toya, Sonya, Neicey, and Precious! You lied to me!"

"I didn't lie about shit! Lisa is facing a federal capital murder case. That's my son's mother. I have to do something. Just like I did when yo baby daddy kidnapped your ass! How is it different? I have to do whatever I can to free her."

"Robert you're right but I can't do this with you. I'll pack our things and go back to my momma's. Just like you have to do this for you son; I have to leave you for my daughters." She wiped her tears and began to walk out the room. "You don't have to leave. I'll leave, but promise me that you'll give me a chance to come back home."

"This will always be your home, and have you forgotten about Precious?"

"Naw I just been busy. I'll email her today."

"I've been emailing her. She knows that you're changing too. You haven't answered any of her calls since all this shit started."

"My phone is off when I'm taking care of business. My Baby girl will understand."

"Cuz tighten up. I'm here for you but just remember that Robert is Cuz but Cuz isn't Robert."

What the hell is that supposed to mean Shree?"

"You'll figure it out, but know this, Cuz isn't welcome here anymore."

That was three months ago. Maria tried to have me live in her brother's old mansion in Miami, but Aza purchased a condo. I met Hector the true man behind the Cuban Cartel. He didn't seem bothered by the fact that Maria brought me in. He showed me the fields where they work the coke from a plant to the white shit that changes lives. Back in the states Maria let me know that El Cappo and the Mexican Cartel were taking over most of the areas in the States. I looked at her and shook my head. "Fuck El Cappo Maria. I'm old school. Shorty dope sells itself."

She shook her head, "Cuz on this level we need whole areas to buy our drugs. I'm talking about moving thousands of kilos. Five thousand a week is no small order."

"We got the whole U.S. right?"

"No we can't move our product in other people's territories."

"Why not?"

"Because it would start a war!"

"You not prepared to go to war?"

"Yes but nobody likes war."

"From what I saw Hector has hundreds of heavily armed men dressed up like they in the army or something. You sell his drugs; he'll support you doing war."

"If I ask for his help it'll make me seem weak. They'll try to replace me. Many of the Cartel members don't like the fact that I'm a woman."

"How many personal bodyguards you got?"

"26, not counting Jackie. Why?"

"Jackie??"

"Yes Jackie!!! She's an Olympic martial artist and knife thrower. She's deadly!"

Waving my hand to cut her off about Jackie, "Anyway, you Hispanic drug lords underestimate us ghetto gangsters."

"No we don't! You guys are not loyal. You turn on each other daily and you're not organized."

"I'm not going to take offense to that but let me pull your coat to something. Who is your biggest buyer here in Miami?"

"Fredro."

"What color is he?"

Black or Haitian, I don't know!"

"What is he copping?"

"Five- hundred kilos a month."

"How many men he got on his team?"

"I don't know. He basically supplies Miami and Orlando? Get to the point! Where are all these questions going?"

"Look you want to get filthy rich and take over the states or what?" Shaking her head, "I knew I shouldn't have involved you!"

"Too late! Look! Call a meeting with everybody you serve, cut down the prices for ten of your best buyers and Ray-Ray from my team included. We need to beef up a hit squad and anybody that goes against the grain dies. We can afford to have the prices that low with Aza helping bring them in now."

"Cuz, El Cappo is catching hell crossing the border. If he can't compete he'll step to us."

"We'll be ready."

"Let's sale them for twelve thousand, ten is too cheap."

"We have to do ten for this to work, trust me. It's still profit. We need everybody to be on our level for this to work. By this time next year we'll be moving over a hundred- thousand bricks a month instead of the bullshit fifteen-thousand that you moving now. Cuba will back to running the coke biz in the U.S."

"You make it sound so easy. A lot of people aren't going to like the change in the prices."

"After I hand pick my hit squad and kill the right people, they won't have a choice." She started stripping out her clothes and walking towards me. "I told you I love it when you talk dirty to me."

Chapter 29 Precious

I've been here in Tallahassee for about 6 months now. I've found my way around, and built my own clique of females. My clique is multi-racial and not based on where you from. It's founded on loyalty, which I feel I'm a good judge of. I had been keeping my eye on Felicia and she had done nothing to make feel she couldn't be trusted. I chunked it up to Mia being jealous of the formation of my crew and trying to crowd my thoughts. My counselor Mrs. Roche is the one who brings in the tobacco and K-2 for me. I personally profit over a thousand dollars a month. Even though I don't need the money I know getting it in here actually helps a lot of the women out that are down for me. Most don't have a lot of support on the outside.

It's sad that so many women have been left stranded by their family and friends just because they came to prison. These women are sisters, daughters, cousins, nieces, girlfriends, and wives to somebody. The visiting room is hardly ever full. I understand that a lot of the women aren't from Florida, but the ones that do get visits get them from their mothers or grandmother's, sisters, or female friends who bring their kids to see them. Most of them are locked up because they caught up in something with a nigga who just moved on to the next bitch.

I thought they were hating on me when I would tell them about how my man is holding me down and just can't come see me because of his background. Lately I've began to think that Cuz may have moved on himself. He hasn't been emailing or answering his calls. It hurts really bad because he's all I have left. Shree is the only person I still talk to and it's made us grow closer. I've actually forgiven her for the snake move she did to have a child. She's been telling me that she and Cuz aren't together anymore and that he's involved with Ricky's sister and some Arab bitch in order to get Lisa out of jail.

Shree wants me to be mad at him too but she doesn't know him or understand him like I do. I know he's going to do whatever it takes to get Lisa out, but I don't think he understands how hard it is to beat the FEDs. I also know that because of him I'm plugged in here so instead of crying and stressing him out about why is not in contact; I'm going to focus on surviving in here and being the leader he would expect me to be. If we would have had some of the women in here on our team, we would have really ran shit. I got two military bitches I cliqued with in here and they are not joke.

Missy loves guns and was a sniper. She can name so many rifles and most I've never even heard of. She says she can make silencers and everything. She grew up hunting with her grandfather at the age of 10. Being a pretty, blonde haired white girl from Wisconsin, she had to fight off a lot of sexual harassment in the military. When one of her superiors tried to use his rank to get his feel on, she shot at him. She missed on purpose, but that didn't stop them from kicking her out and landing her a federal prison sentence for three years. I promised to make sure when she gets out that Cuz puts her back on her feet because her grandfather died while she's been serving her time.

If Cuz is back in the streets, he's going to need some help. Me, Neicey, Sonya, Toya, and Shree were loyal to him and would kill or die for him as Toya, Sonya, and Neicey did. With someone like Missy and China Doll he'll really do his thing. China Doll is from Dallas, Texas. She was a chemist and explosive expert who received a dishonorable discharge when she was caught with enough C-4 in her personal belongings to knock down the Sears Tower. She says her military ex-boyfriend was the one who stole the stuff but she didn't tell. He didn't hold her down and keep it real with her. He never sent her a letter, not even one money order. Her entire family disowned her because her father was ex-military and she brought shame on the whole family. She gets out a little before Missy.

China Doll is 25 but can pass for a teenager. She's 5 foot 2, pretty as a doll, with a sexy petite shape. She's called China Doll because of her beautiful slanted eyes. We have been cellmates for about four months and this little sexy, chocolate chick has me thinking I'm fully gay by the way I lust for her. Needless to say, everyone knows she's mine and vice versa. I'm sending her home to Cuz. She will run my shop and live in one of my apartments. I talked so much about Cuz that China Doll believes he's her man already. I really need to talk to him. I don't understand why his phone has been off. I quit trying to call because it made me mad hearing the recording about the person I'm calling is unavailable.

On Saturdays I usually hang with my crew, smoke K-2, and talk shit. Rosa and a few other girls play on the volleyball team, so me and the rest of the crew go to watch and support. That'll keep me busy and my mind off things until *Power* comes on tonight on *Starz*. "Count time ladies! All inmates report to your cells." A C.O. said over the loud speaker. The C.O.'s walked past our cell and counted us so China Doll and I sat back down on the bottom bunk. "Baby girl if you haven't heard from our man how you know he'll be ready for me when I get out?"

"He'll come around and if he doesn't, I'll still make sure you are okay. Depending on what Missy wants to do, you guys can stay in one of my apartments."

"I don't mind living with her but you the only woman I want to be with." That made me smile and I kissed her. We heard the C.O.'s keys jiggling so we stopped before she made it back by our cell. She stopped right in front of us. "Jones?"

"Yeah."

"You have a visit when count clears."

"Okay." I was super happy and surprised.

China Doll jumped up hugging me. She seemed more excited than I was. "Is it Daddy?"

"Calm down! No he's not even on my visiting list." As soon as I said that I thought about the phony attorney visit I had in Oklahoma. "Naw it's more than likely Shree."

"Well that's still good isn't it?" I knew she was pressing me because she needed a place to stay and a job when she got out.

"Yeah it's all good China. I told you I got you. I'm going to take care of you." She kissed me again.

Walking into the visiting room, I was looking for Shree and the kids but I didn't see them. I almost passed out when I saw the finest man in the world wearing jeans, a black v-neck t-shirt, and some black and white Air Forces. His iced-out Cuban link chain made the lights dance off his HB emblem. This was my man, the man I would spend eternity in hell for. I felt like a star knowing he was here to see me. His neatly trimmed facial hair and the waves in his hair would make you think he was mixed or something. His body standing about six feet talk with serious muscle definition had every bitch in the visiting room checking him out, even the C.O.'s.

He stood up, holding his arms open for me to walk into them. Being embraced by him was like walking into Heaven and the Polo cologne he was wearing was driving me crazy. I just buried my head in his chest and closed the world out. He grabbed my butt and lifted my head up by my chin, looked me in the eyes, and kissed me. We were allowed a kiss when our visit started and one when it was over. I must have forgotten we were even on a visit because he was always able to make me horny just by kissing me. I began grind on him and reaching for his dick. He stopped me, "Baby girl you gone get us kicked out the visiting room before the visit even starts."

I smiled then sat down across from him. He had pops, popcorn, pizza, and chicken wings already waiting from the vending machine. "I didn't know what you wanted so I got some of everything."

"I'm cool. I'm not even hungry. I'm glad you're here."

"Come on man, like I wasn't going to make a way to see my Baby girl." That brought tears to my eyes. He sat up on the edge of his seat and wiped my tears. "What's wrong Precious?" I shook my head, "Nothing." I tried my best to smile but I started crying again. This time he got up and hugged me. The C.O. started walking in our direction because he wasn't supposed to do it. "Daddy you can't touch me like this, they will kill our visit."

He stepped back and turned to the C.O. telling her it wouldn't happen again. "Baby girl, tell me what's wrong for real! We supposed to be able to tell each other anything." I was feeling ashamed, looking at the ground. "I thought you left me." I looked back at him and he had a look of disappointment on his face. "I'm sorry Baby girl. I've been busy. I've been flying all over the world. I had to make this Princess from Kuwait fall in love with me to help someone out in order to get Lisa out. "I know. Shree told me. It's just that you didn't even email and your phone was never on, and then hearing you mixed up with Maria!"

"Precious that will never happen again. I'm so sorry. I'm doing things on a level that I never dreamed of doing. I'm seeing places I never knew existed. I will never forget about you though. I promise you that, one day you will see them too. I'm going to get you the fuck out of here."

"I know daddy but honestly I'm cool down her. I got my own clique of females. Oh before I forget! Two of my girls will be getting out soon. I know you can use them and I promised them I would take care of them when they got out! I need you to look out for them and put them on our team until I get out."

"Oh yeah? I'm feeling you! Look at you, now that's my Baby girl!"

We started laughing. "I miss you so much and China Doll, keep her until I get out by all means."

"That's your lil thang-thang up in here?"

"Yup! She's sexy! Watch when you see her, and she can blow shit up!" We spent the rest of the visit talking and catching up. Then he told me about Aza. The one Shree calls the Arab bitch. He let me know that she knows about me and how he's beginning to trust her. He also explained that once me and Lisa are out that he was going to have to make some serious moves to get his life back in order, and make sure his family is safe.

"So are you saying we may have to leave the country?"

"Yes, if we truly want out the game! The type of stuff I'm dealing with now is for life. We gone eventually end up dead or all in jail."

141

Three o'clock came fast and our visit was over. We stood up and kissed again but before he let go of me I had to ask him, "How did you get in to visit me?"

"Your counselor put me on your visiting list."

"So you can come see me whenever?"

"Yup baby, I'll be back but it'll be in like another month. I have to tighten things up to make sure everybody safe. I need to know that I can take on whoever or whatever comes at me."

"I understand."

"I know you do. I'll email you as much as possible. I just can't be caught slipping because I'm playing on a very serious level. If I lose, we all lose."

Chapter 30 D.A Cruiz

I was pacing around my office floor sweating. I had just watched a DVD of myself engaged in sex with a minor and another scene of me choking a 14 year old boy to death. To add insult to injury there were multiple clips of me receiving payments from the late Ricky Santana, the Cuban drug lord. There was another of me naked in bed with a young Hispanic boy as I bragged about how was going to win the Governor's Mansion with the help of Ricky; as I snorted a line of coke then passed it to my young lover.

The package was delivered to my office this morning along with a typed up note telling me that the case against Lisa better disappear, or the same video footage would make headline news. "I thought this shit died with Ricky! Just as I'm trying to avenge his death, the same shit is being held over my head!" The phone rang and after it rang eight times it stopped and began to ring again. "Hello!" It was my secretary. "Mr. Cooly is here to see you. Should I send him in?"

"Fuck!"

"Um sir, are you okay?" Realizing my slip I tried to turn it professional. "Yes, send him in Ms. Scott and I apologize for my outburst."

"No problem Mr. Cruiz." Cooly walked into my office carrying two folders. I was still holding the manila folder that held my life's fate. Cooly was overly excited. "Cruiz I got it!" Cooly said as he ruffled through papers in his folders. "Here it is! Remember the White Chrysler that was seen on camera outside Mrs. Green's shop?" I was in a daze but he continued. "Well after running a check at the B.M.V. guess who owned a white Chrysler at the time?"

"What?"

"Yes Lisa did! Yeah we got her along with the witness that saw her running through the alley and dumping the gun at the time. The Grand Jury will give up the indictment. After she's officially charged, I'm sure she will cooperate against Robert Wilson."

"No!"

"What? What are you talking about Cruiz? This is what we been looking for!"

I was quickly trying to think of something before I answered. "James, she didn't do it, couldn't have done it."

"Really? Please enlighten me."

"Look she's a mother of two and a successful business owner."

"That's it? That's all you have?"

"I know it's not her. Damn it James, just let this go!"

I could see the surprise and confusion on his face. "You're starting to sound like her lawyer. Look Cruiz, this is the same case you told me to take the gloves off for. Now you want to lay down with no solid reason?"

"I'm the D.A. here and I took an oath to uphold justice. Attacking a mother of two to take down her son's father isn't right and it's not what justice stands for."

Cooly just stared at me and then at the envelope in my hand. I self-consciously put the envelope behind my leg.

"Cruiz what the fuck is going on here?"

"Nothing, this is nothing."

"I'm not talking about the envelope that you're acting like you're trying to hide, but the sudden change concerning the case!"

"James you're going to be the D.A. in Florida soon, very soon in fact. There's going to come a time when you're just going to have to make decisions that everyone in your office don't agree with or understand; but you are the representative of justice in that office."

"So you're dismissing the case?"

"Yes!"

"With prejudice or without?"

"With!"

"You got to be kidding me!"

Standing up to leave Cooly threw the folders on my desk. "I pray that you go over everything in these folders and study this case before you make up your mind. I don't know what's in that envelope you're hold, but I have a feeling it's what's clouding your judgement. For the record our job as United States District Attorney's is to protect the public from crime, terror, and things that go against it right?" He walked out my office and slammed the door.

After Cooly left my office I made the necessary call to have Lisa released from the county jail. I then called her lawyer. "Donald Jefferson, Attorney at Law."

"Yes! This is D.A. Cruiz from the Prosecutors office in Indianapolis. May I speak with Mr. Jefferson? Tell him it's urgent."

"Hold on a second."

"Hello, Cruiz?"

"Yes, Mr. Jefferson. I'm personally calling you to inform you that all charges against your client will be dropped, but I'm requesting a private meeting with her son's father."

"I don't know if I can arrange that. I represent Lisa."

"Come on now Don, cut the bullshit. I know he bank rolled her defense. Tell him to call me within the hour and arrange a meeting with just us. There's no need for a lawyer."

"I'll see what I can do."

Chapter 31 Cuz

"Oh yeah? His fat ass wants to have a meeting with me huh?"

"That's what he said and he said no need for lawyers. What's that about?" I laughed. "Nothing, so when is she getting out?"

"Sometime today. Maybe five or six."

"Call the fat bastard and tell him to meet me at The Capital Grille in downtown Indianapolis about 2 p.m. tomorrow."

"Will do, by the way Ms. Jones appeal has been answered somewhat. I'm scheduled for oral arguments next week."

"Is that good?"

"Hell yeah. She was a juvenile when they indicted her, and the federal agents never identified themselves as officers before they pulled their guns. It's my argument that the girls were defending themselves, thinking they were getting robbed. If things go right, she will be released."

"Don if you pull that off, I'll give you a hundred- thousand dollar bonus."

"Cuz you working with the best, you might be out a hundred g's."

"I hope so."

I hung up the phone and got back to my meeting. "Excuse me fellas, now where were we?" Jessie, James, and

Ray-Ray were sitting around the bar in my office. Ray-Ray spoke up, "You were saying something about murder and five hundred bricks a week."

"Oh Yeah! Look. I'm back down, but this time things are way bigger than before. Now I'm more than likely going to be in this shit for life, but I need my loyal soldiers."

"Cuz we here with you all day every day, what the lick read? You know me and mine are ready." Jessie said with confidence. I nodded my head. "Hold on before you agree. Look ya'll been getting money for a minute without me. Together ya'll get about twenty bricks a month with Ray-Ray getting half of that right?" James looked offended. "What's your point?"

"I'm getting to it. I want to kill the person ya'll getting the work from and so on down the line." I waited to see how they reacted to what I had just said.

They all sat silent waiting to hear what else I had to say. "Ya'll don't seem bothered by killing your connect. I'm little insulted." Ray-Ray chimed in. "Because that's all he is, a connect, plus I been hearing he's the want sent that bitch to set up Wayne to get wacked. That was my ace. I can give a fuck less if my connect lives or dies. They sure don't give a fuck if I live or die. That's not the case with you Cuz."

"Damn Ray-Ray I thought you was more about the business side of things."

"I am. It's like this Cuz, I peeped that even though we get our work from different connects, all our shit comes from Javier. He got them low budget used car lots in Gary.

"Didn't he use to by from Wayne back in the day?"

"Yeah, he used to get five bricks then but now he's the man up this way. I'm telling you I think he got Wayne. It's been a burning feeling I've had. He got the whole Midwest sewed up now, shipping cars loaded with bricks and Mexican tart throughout the Midwest."

I sat back in my seat and thought about what I was just told. "Jessie I'm going to give you some money to buy twenty bricks from him. If he ask why you buying so many let him know your old team is working together again. Flip the bricks and ya'll need to find out as much as you can about Javier's operation. I need ya'll to pull all your men together because after we hit him, we gone find and hit the Javier of the South and East Coast. I got people in those areas already on it."

"Damn Cuz what you on?"

"James I got a direct Cartel connect, and I'm going to need Ray-Ray to be the Javier in this area. Jessie and James I'm a need ya'll and as many niggas that's bout that gun play as we can get to help us pull this shit off. I'm trying to move six thousand bricks a week through the states. Next month we're hitting everybody that's in the way. They might rename it Bloody May."

I gave them two hundred g's to get things started and told them keep it among us; but to also be ready to strike when I give the word.

Chapter 32 Lisa

Me and Me-Me were chilling in our cell for 3 o'clock shift change and count. When the C.O. walked by our cell he doubled back. "Mrs. Rayan pack your shit, you are out of here after count." My heart nearly jumped out my chest. I thought he was bullshitting, but if they had somehow fucked up and let me out I was getting my babies and running straight for the border. "Can this really be happening?"

"Girl he don't look like he playing. Maybe the FEDs still don't have enough to indict you."

"Yea but it still seems like a dream."

"Fuck that! Grab your pictures, your letters, and paperwork and get the hell up out of here." I was shaking as I grabbed my things. "Bitch quit being scared. Hell if you don't want to go, I'll go!"

"Can you make a phone call and tell my assistant Kim that they letting me out and to please come pick me up? Here's her number and here's my home number. Call me. I'm going to be sure to send you some money."

"Girl you ain't got to lie to me. Just get out and take care of your babies and if you really want to help me stop by my mother's house from time to time and look out for my son."

"I promise I will." We hugged. The C.O. unlocked the cell letting me know it was time to go. Me-Me walked me to the front door of our section. When I was in the hallway and the C.O. shut the big steel door to the section I heard Me-Me yell, "Ride some dick for me!"

It took three hours going through the process of getting released from the jail. When I made it outside Kim, Mrs. Wilson, and Lil Kris were out front waiting on me. Lil Kris took off running to me. He damn near knocked me down when he jumped up in to my arms. It felt so good to embrace my baby. I held him so tight and never wanted to let him go. Leaving my babies is something I'll never do again if I can help it. I was disappointed in not seeing Lil Rob or his dad but I was so happy to be out that I brushed it off.

Kim walked up and hugged me, "Welcome home Boss Lady." We both laughed. "Thank you Kim. I don't know what I would have done without you.
"Ah well hopefully we'll never find out." Mrs. Wilson hugged me next. "Baby it's so good to have you back."
"Why was Kris being bad?"
"Oh no! That's my baby. It's just been so long since I had to help get somebody ready for school. Hell one morning I even called him Robert thinking I was getting my baby up for school

again." We all laughed. "Speaking of Robert, where's my Robert?"

"Girl you know how kids are. Come on. Let's get you some real food to eat. Big Rob is going to meet us and he's bringing my grandbaby with him."

Chapter 33 Cuz

I couldn't believe that this little nigga had his phone off. It was sending me straight to voice mail and I had told him about that shit. I wanted to give him the heads up that his mom was home since I had been letting him stay at the house alone. I could only imagine what he had Lisa's house looking like. I used my key to let myself in. I was surprised to see the house was actually clean. I was just about to call his name when a young, belly t-shirt wearing thick, brown-skinned chic came from the bedroom heading for the bathroom. She didn't see me so she kept talking.

"Come on ya'll get up! You know I got to meet my date downtown at 5." Then another one came out the same room naked as the day she was born. "Well then bitch you better make room in the shower." She turned back towards the room and yelled, "L.C. boy come on, get up, and let's get ready!" "Trina you don't run shit here. This is my house. I'm the man up in here. Just go get in the shower and I'm coming." He came walking out the room and that's when he saw me standing there and stiffened. He froze up looking in my direction and that's when the girl name Trina looked my way and jumped. Trying to cover as much as she could of her body with her hands she spoke, "Hello!"

"Hello to you too." The other girl in the shower yelled out L.C. come and get in the shower, we don't have all day." The girl named Trina ran off to the bathroom." I just kept looking at Lil Cuz. "Um let me go put some shorts on."

"Please do. I ain't seen you naked since I changed your pamper."

After a few minute he came out in some shorts and a t-shirt. I was sitting in the living room shaking my head. He was trying to be me and replicate everything I did. I didn't know if I should feel bad or proud. "Tell the girls to get dressed and come into the living room." He went into the bathroom and came back out and sat across from me smiling. I was trying to play like I was mad at him. I guess I was supposed to be mad but I started laughing. "Nigga you know you fucking up right?" He hunched his shoulders. "Now you ain't got shit to say/" "What am I supposed to say?" That made me laugh even harder.

"Can you imagine if Lisa would have walked in on all of this?"

His eyes got big. "Tell your two girlfriends not be scared and come on out here."

"Trina and Kayla?"

"Yeah??" They both said in unison.

"Ya'll hurry up. My dad wants to talk to ya'll."

They came out the room and into the living room looking embarrassed. "Trina and Kayla, is it? Look don't be afraid of me just don't lie to me about nothing." They both nodded their heads. "Ya'll been staying here or you all just spent a couple nights?" Neither answered me. They both looked at my son. "They've been staying with me."

"I figured that, well your momma is out." He had the biggest smile. "For real?"

"Yeah, now here's the thing, you know damn well that girl gone have a fit if she knew ya'll was all staying here in her house; so I'm a take you to go meet up with her and I need ya'll to clean the fuck out this house to the point that she won't know other women were staying here. Can ya'll do that?" They nodded their heads. "Alright yall got like two hours. Ya'll got a car?"

Kayla spoke up. "I do."

"Okay good. Pack ya'll shit up and take it to this address. Here are the keys and this is the number to the house alarm system." Trina looked at the address. "This house is on the north side!!"

"You got a problem with the north side?"

"Oh no, it's just I know this area. All the houses over there are nice. I mean very nice."

"That's how my dad gets down. Now get up and get things moving because if my mama would have walked in here all hell would have broken loose." I shook my head at him again.

By the time we made it to the restaurant they were already finished eating. Lisa smiled at us then began shaking her head. "Why you shaking your head like you ain't happy to see your Robs?"

"Dad she's fronting." He walked to where she was sitting and gave her a long big hug. "I missed you ma."

"I can't tell! When the last time you came to see me?" He looked scared then looked up at me. She continued her rant. "You've been having hoes in my house? Yeah you thought I didn't know!" I jumped in. "Man cool all that out. You home now and you're with family. Show us some love instead of fussing." She folded her arms and cut her eyes at us.

I gave him a look letting him know to follow my move. We both went in and hugged her on both sides and kissed her on her cheeks. "We love you too," After dinner was over I asked my mom to let Lil Kris stay one more night at her house. Lil Kris started pouting. "I wanna go home with my momma."

"Ooh baby I'll be to get you tomorrow when you get out of school and we'll spend the whole day together." She hugged him as he nodded his head and wiped his tears. "See you at work soon Boss Lady." Kim said walking towards her car. "I'll be in day after tomorrow."

"Come on Lil Rob so I can drop you off to your friends and take your mom home."

"Cool."

"Ya'll better keep my shit tight, don't fuck up my crib."

"I won't."

"What crib, what yall talking about? Robert what's going on?"

"Nothing, but our son growing up."

After we got back to Lisa's house I was happy to see Lil Rob's girlfriends had cleaned up good. Sitting in the living room I told Lisa about how I got her out and that I had to get back in the game to do so. I told her about losing Shree because of it but didn't regret my decision. "Well just stop selling drugs now that I'm out!"

"It's not that simple. I'm dealing directly with the Cartel. I've been traveling all across the world while you've been locked up. These people will kill my whole family so I'm in this til I die or go to prison." She held her head down and then looked back up with teary eyes. "I'm so sorry, I didn't-"I cut her off. "Baby you didn't do nothing wrong. She dropped her head again. I moved closer to her and lifted her head up by her chin. "Lisa look at me. Baby I was made for this shit. I love this. This is what I've always wanted to do; now I'm forced to be a boss but I was born to do this. Whoever thought a nigga from East Hammond would be the biggest American Gangster ever?"

She looked at me deep in my eyes trying to read me. "I need you to know who I am and what I'm doing so if I ever call you and I tell you to drop everything, and then do what I tell you without even thinking twice. Can I depend on you?" She closed her eyes and answered yes. I kissed her and she moaned out and lost her breath, then her body went limp letting me know to take the lead.

Chapter 34 Cuz

Lisa and I sexed all night from the living room, to the tub, and all in her bedroom til we fell asleep. In the morning I left to go meet up with this fat fuck district attorney. I called Mr. Smith to make sure that he had the spot bugged and ready to video tape the whole meeting. I arrived at the restaurant a little after two and to my surprise Cruiz was already there. He waved me over to his table. As I walked over I quickly tried to scan the place for Mr. Smith, needless to say I didn't find him.

When I made it to his table he attempted to stand. "That won't be necessary, stay seated." I took the seat across from him. "So what's this meeting all about?" He took a break from his porter house steak and baked potato and gave me a half ass laugh while trying to finish chewing his food, and shaking his head at me. "I called you to meet with me to let you know-." He was interrupted by the young white waiter. "Excuse me sir, will you be eating anything?"

"Naw, just bring me a mocha chocolate ice coffee with extra sugar. I won't be staying long." He wrote down my order.

"Will there be anything else Mr. Cruiz?"

"No that's it kid. Put his coffee on my bill." When the waiter walked off I noticed an extremely fat white man paying too much attention to us or maybe he was feeling funny thinking that I was watching him. He had four plates of food at his table.

I shook my head at the greedy obese man. Cruiz took notice of the man also, "People like him make me want to watch what I eat." I just nodded my head. "Now Mr. Wilson you know exactly why we're having this here meet."
"No, can't say that I do. Fill me in." He started whispering in a threatening tone. "Look here you black son of a bitch. I got your package in the mail yesterday morning and for the record that's it. That's all. I'm not going to let you hold this shit over my head like Ricky did and I know you had something to do with his death." I just stared at him, which made him even madder. "I won't be pushed around and used. You want to play ball with the big boys? I'll make you disappear from the world as you know it, now if any of those things from that disk ever gets out you can kiss you black ass goodbye."

The waiter returned with my ice coffee. "Here you go sir."
"Thanks." The waiter walked off again. I took a sip of my drink and then opened up four sugar packs, poured it, stirred it, and then tasted it again. Smacking my lips, "Now that's how I like it." He got frustrated. "Did you hear anything I just said?" I smiled at him, took another sip, and swallowed it down. I was

looking at my cup as I truly enjoyed my drink. "Well answer me got damn it!"

I laughed a little. "Victor who in the fuck do you think you talking to? I'm not Ricky and I damn sure ain't no young faggot ass boy you fucking with." I looked him dead in his eyes so that he could see that I was far from the scary type. "Look here you fat fag, you gone do just what the fuck I tell your ass to do. The only way that disk gets out is if you don't. Right now all I want you to do is make sure me and my people stay off the FEDs radar."

"That's it?"

"For now and for the record, I'm not as selfish as you may think." I pulled an envelope out my pocket with 10 G's in it. He grabbed it and looked inside. "That's 10 G's and a number for you to call, they'll hook your faggot ass up with all the punks you want. It'll be on the hush hush."

He nervously put the envelope in his inside suit jacket pocket. "Tha-Than- Thank you Robert." I shook my head. "Call me Cuz, and remember Victor you work for me now." I got up and left him at the table. I was in a hurry to get to my phone so I can text Mr. Smith. I couldn't believe he left me hanging while I was dealing with a Federal United States district attorney. I sent him a text. "*Where u @?*"

"Still in here with four plates recording Cruiz."

"☺ *U my #1 Mr. Smith!*" I couldn't believe it! He was wearing the fat suit. That was one hell of an investment. I walked to my car laughing.

Chapter 35 Precious

I'm happy and sad at the same time because my girl China Doll is leaving. We made pizzas and all types of other food that we stole out the kitchen yesterday. We sexed all night and never went to sleep. I know I was being selfish because I wanted last night to last forever, but time never stops and the sun will always rise. Rosa, Tammy, Missy, and I walked her to Receiving and Departure. Everybody gave her hugs but then walked off to give us some alone time.

I tried my best to be strong by thinking what would Cuz do right now; but when she looked at me all teary eyed I shed a few tears as well. "Baby girl you want me to blow something up and come right back?" That made me laugh. "You so crazy. China go ahead and go home. I don't know how he got your halfway house suspended but remember to take care of my man. I really love him and don't get it any trouble because I can't wait to sleep with the both of you at the same time."
"I'll do whatever you ask. I love you."
"I love you too. Now hurry up and don't keep our man waiting too long. Remember suck his dick for me on the way home."
"Ok."

The guard opened the door letting her know it was time for her to go. We hugged and tongue kissed right in front of the C.O. Hell! I didn't care if they put me in the hole or not. We broke our kiss and said our goodbyes. China Doll walked out the prison leaving me mad and heartbroken. I already heard how bitches in here were waiting on China to leave, thinking they had a chance to get wifed up next. That shit wasn't happening. At least not while I still had hope on getting out; as long as Cuz is alive I'll always have hope of getting out one day.

Chapter 36 Cuz

Baby girl's lil girlfriend has been home with me for a couple weeks now. I can see why Precious chose her. China is not only attractive with clear chocolate skin; she's sexy, obedient, and submissive. It kind of throws me off sometimes. It shocked me at how loyal she is to Precious. She not only emails her all day and talks to her on the phone but she won't engage in any type of sex with Aza, Jackie, or Maria. Aza is actually attracted to China but China refuses to let Aza touch her. The most she'll do is have sex with me. Every time Aza tries, China straight out lets her know that it's Baby girls pussy.

I was able to get her supervise release transferred to Indianapolis thanks to my new worker D.A. Cruiz. It's to the point that China doesn't have to report as long as she doesn't get arrested outside of Nap. I set her up with an account in a bogus name so she'll be able to order the things she says she needs to blow up whatever I want her to. This girl is an electronic genius. As sexy and fine as she is, it's hard to believe she can be so deadly. She looks like she wouldn't hurt a fly but this little sex kitten will blow your whole damn block off the map.

I purchased her a nice place outside of Indianapolis in Zionsville, Indiana with enough land that she could practice blowing up shit without alerting her neighbors or the police. Aza has been spending time in her country lately but she instructed her personal pilot to fly the shipments in that I need. I told her that for the next couple weeks I was going to be very busy waging war in the states.

Chapter 37 Cuz

"Cuz this nigga Javier really got shit on lock up this way." Jesse said as Ray-Ray chimed in. "Yeah fam he even got a Gary police officer on his team. He been having him pull niggas over but not arresting them. I heard Javier got a farm out in Valpo somewhere where they torturing and killing niggas."

"Fuck him! I don't pull over for the opps anyway!"

"James you crazy." I laughed.

"On some real shit tho. I kept laughing. "I know and that's why you spend so much money buying new cars." He hunched his shoulders. "Alright ya'll on some real shit if we kill Javier who you think is going to step up in his place?"

"Lupe! That's his right hand man."

"So that means he got to go too. Jesse is there a chance that we can kill'em both at the same time? Maybe even fuck around take their bricks?"

"Cuz it's like this, they get bullshit cars sent up this way from Texas loaded with coke and boy. Javier owns used car lots in Ohio, Missouri, Iowa, Illinois, Michigan, Wisconsin, and Minnesota. I mean pretty much he got the mad ass middle sewed up! He uses his lot in Gary as the main base because it's in the middle of all the Midwest states. I'm telling you Cuz this nigga is super major."

"Yeah Cuz Jesse's right! How in the hell am I supposed to be the next Javier?"

"Ray-Ray when I knock this muthafucka off the map, there's going to be a drought so serious that the dope boys gonna come looking. When word gets out that you got them for fifteen, Javier's people are going to spend that money too. Just like ya'll didn't give a fuck if he lived or died, them others are going to be the same way. If not I'll deal with them too. Fellas in this game we play somebody is always waiting to take the next man's place."

James asked, "So we gone kill Javier and Lupe, steal their product, and then turn around and sell it super cheap?"

"Naw, yall listen up! I just thought about it, fuck taking they bricks. We gone blow them and their dope away and sell our own shit. I'm getting them so cheap that once Ray-Ray is able to sell five-hundred a week I'm a put ya'll on a twenty-five thousand dollar a week salary; but we got to stick together and everybody gotta play their part. When one of us lacking, we all suffer. The core of our team starts with us and before it's over all ya'll will be running different coasts, making a half mil a week." Ray-Ray shook his head. "Cuz you talking big numbers and a lot of big boy shit."

"Remember when you couldn't afford to buy an ounce for five-hundred when I first met you?" He smiled. "Yeah!" "Remember when I told you if you stick with me I'm a make you a rich nigga?" They all nodded their heads. "Well I make sure my word is bond. Just see to it that ya'll do the same!" James jumped up. "Man we with you, fuck it! Let's make it happen!"

"That's what I'm talking about! So Jesse when is the best time to visit Javier?"

"The second Sunday of each month he has one of those big trucks carrying cars come to his lot. The truck takes most of those cars off and throughout the week other trucks pull in and take at least one of the cars that were dropped off Sunday. I figure different trucks go to different places in the Midwest to his other lots. We never allowed there second Sunday of the month. They be deep as hell up there, and strapped up ready for war. I ain't a coward, but I don't think he can be hit without bodies being dropped on each end."

I sat back in my leather chair with my hands folded on my chest and my feet kicked up on the desk like I didn't have a care in the world. I shook my head and smiled. "Ye of little faith. Ray I'm a have to show you the difference in killing somebody and robbing someone. I'm not taking his dope. I'm taking his life and his position in the Midwest. As a matter of fact, I don't need ya'll to do nothing else to make this happen. You already did enough. Now just sit back and watch your boy do his thang." I grabbed the phone and dialed China. "China Doll, get ready I need you to test-drive a bunch of cars!"

Chapter 38 Cuz

2 weeks later I sat in a SUV at The Village Shopping mall with China Doll and Jesse looking out the back window with binoculars. "Jess are you sure that this truck comes today?"

"Man, the last two months it's been coming in around one or two in the afternoon." Looking at my watch I said, "Fam it is damn near three thirty!"

"That's him right there pulling up. That's Javier."

"In the dirty jeans and cowboy hat?"

"Yea that's him." A red Tahoe pulled in. "Who is that in the Tahoe?"

"That's Lupe. Man it don't look like the truck coming so fuck the truck, but we can kill two birds with one stone."

"I might have to. China baby you sure you can blow the whole car lot up and everybody in it?"

"Hell yes. I'm a professional. I can do this shit in my sleep. All cars will blow up in the direction of the office. The restroom and soda machine will blow up everything in the office. No survivors, no mess, very clean."

She pulled out her Smartphone. "All I do is call this number and detonate the bombs.

"Fuck it! Do it." She began dialing the number on her phone. Jesse grabbed her shoulder. "Hold up! Stop!"

"What's the matter?"

"Look there goes the truck." A semi truck came through the light on 35th and Grant pulling three tier level trailers headed for the car lot. "Wait until the truck is on the lot."

"Man Cuz, I don't understand why we can't jack the truck. There might be a thousand keys on that truck."

"Because I'm sending a message, plus we have thousands of keys ourselves."

The truck pulled onto the lot and they locked the gate behind the truck. We watched as everyone came out to greet the driver. After the truck was pulled close to the garage a Gary police car pulled up to the gate. "Damn what the fuck is this? If we kill the police then shit gone get hot as hell out here."

"Don't call the number yet?

"Naw baby hold on."

"Cuz fuck that nigga, he's the dirty cop that works for him."

"Yeah?" Jesse took the binoculars to get a better look. "Hell yeah! That's that bitch!"

"Fuck it. China blow that muthafucka up!" She pushed a few numbers on her phone and a series of loud booms echoed through the air as the ground shook. It sounded like we were in the middle of a world war.

Jesse jumped every time a bomb went off. The shit was so loud that I even jumped a few times but China just sat smiling like a proud mother seeing her child's first graduation.

Chapter 39 Cuz

Everything was going according to plan. Ray-Ray was sitting at the top of the dope game in the Midwest. We only had to take out Javier's people in Ohio because they were family. Everybody else came onboard with no problem, especially after I had body parts of Javier's cousin in Ohio sent to their car lots, plus our prices were cheaper. Precious other home girl Missy was now home from prison. She wasn't interested in hooking up with me sexually which was cool. Her only concern in life was getting her grandfather's farm land back up in Wisconsin.

Her grandfather was the only family she had and when he died while she was locked up she wasn't able to pay off the back taxes. I dropped a couple hundred grand for Missy to get her land back and make some upgrades. Since then she's been truly grateful and loyal. Missy is a true marksman with any type of firearm but rifles are her specialty. I helped finance a state of the art shooting range for her on her land, where she helps train my soldiers. My team has expanded majorly. We have no problems getting the coke in because the Cartel themselves have been investing in other planes that fly under the radar. They drop loads off in different places that their own people pick up and deliver to me. Now I'm getting twice as much coke as before.

Chapter 40 Cuz

Today is my off day sort of to say. I decided to spend the day with Shree and my daughters. It was surprising to me to find out that Shree moved back home with her mom in Merrillville, so I had to visit with them over there. I got there a little after 4 p.m. Edwina and LaNeice were excited to see me. When Shree let me in and Edwina saw me she ran out the kitchen and jumped straight into my arms yelling, "Daddy!" "Hey baby how's my favorite girl?" It made her blush. "I'm good."

"Did you miss me as much as I missed you?"

"Yes!" Shree went to get LaNeice. When my baby girl saw me her eyes lit up like diamonds. I held my little angle while Edwina was still wrapped around me by my waist.

I kissed her on her forehead! "Hey princess." She giggled. "Hi dad!" My heart was filled with so much joy and love. Thirty minutes later we were seated at the dinner table. Shree and her mother went all out and cooked a full course meal. Her mother asked that we all hold hands and bow our heads in preparing to bless the food. "Edwina you want to show your father how much of a big girl you are by saying grace?" She took a breath. "God is great. God is good. Let us thank him for this food." We all said, "Amen."

"I'm not done yet! God I want to thank you for bringing my daddy to see us, Amen." Hearing that almost broke me down. I had to wipe away the tear that tried to drop before anybody saw it. I missed my kids. Shree gave me a look letting me know that I was wrong for being away for so long.

We ate and I kicked it with my babies as Edwina told me about school, church, and her favorite songs. After about an hour and half Shree laid LaNeice down for a nap and told Edwina to go wash up then watch T.V. in her room. She started pouting, "I wanna stay with my daddy."

"After I finish talking to your momma I'll come and watch T.V. with you, okay?" She smiled and ran off. After the kids were gone Cheri asked me, "Robert I don't want to get in your personal affairs, but I'm not blind. What I mean by this is I believe I know what you're doing now as far as living in the street life." I looked at Shree and she gave me a look like she didn't know where her mother was going with the conversation.

"Robert I'm more hip then Shree believes I am. I went through a lot myself to get to where I am. Shree's father was also a hustler." Shree's eyes got big. I guess this was the first time she was hearing this too. "I see you over there looking shocked. I never told you about your father because I didn't want you to know that part of life. Robert what I want to ask you is why hustle illegally, taking dangerous chances daily of going to prison or getting killed, when you already have more than what you need?"

I couldn't believe that I was about to have this conversation with Shree's mother, but as I thought about it, I figured she needed to know something as to why her daughter was home. "Cheri, I don't know what all Shree has told you about me, but my situation isn't as simple as having things and making money." I began to explain to her all about my five years in prison. How I felt like everybody I took care of and loved left me hanging. How I swore to myself that I'd never go broke again, and how heartbroken I was when my son's mother left me flat and dry. To bury the hurt I redirected all my love and focus to hustling in jail and making plans to expand that hustle once I was out.

"So Cheri when I dedicated myself to the hustle, hustling brought me everything I ever dreamed about while I was in prison and most definitely when I came home. I was able to get the nice rides, a beautiful home, women, respect, and I was able to help those who depend on me. What makes a man is being able to provide for his family and making sacrifices. I made it out the streets but my loyalty to my family has pulled me back in."

I looked at Shree and took a deep breath before continuing. "I was at a crossroad. My first love, Lisa, was facing charges that could put her in prison the rest of her life. I was presented with an option to marry my second love for life, until I die, through the good and the bad, to free her. I love my son more than life itself and I can only imagine how he feels about his mother. There was no way that I wouldn't take an opportunity that could free her. Shree was just looking dumb founded, again like it was first time she heard me explain the situation; or maybe it was her first hearing me break it down like that.

"I understand how you feel, but with me being a God fearing person it wouldn't be right for me not to say that if you believe in God as I know you do, you have to know and understand that the devil and evil exist also. The devil will pull the strings that he knows will move you. That's what makes temptation tempting, but when he comes we have to fight his urges with prayer and faith. I knew your situation was something serious because Shree ran back home to me instead of staying at that big beautiful home you gave her."

She grabbed my hands. "Robert I want you to know that I've become one of your biggest supporters. I was there though out Precious's trail and sentencing. LaToya was my sister's daughter. I also know Sonya and Neicey's people so I went through that hurt with you all. What I'm trying to tell you is death surrounds you as long as you continue to live this life. Each time you walked away from this life, rather by choice or force, you always lost something or somebody close to you."

"So you saying I shouldn't ever quit?"

"No not at all! I'm saying the opposite. God has a plan for you but Satan wants you because you're a leader and others will follow you. When you're living illegal, selling drugs or whatever else you're into you're doing the devils work. God tries to pull you way. The first time he sent you to prison and Satan took your son's mother out of your life to harden your heart. No one sent you any money to truly make you bitter. When you were freed you came out running to do the devil's work just as he knew you would. He's setting you up son. He paid you a lot of money and surrounded you with flashy things. The leader in you emerged and you had my daughter plus four other young women following you down the road of destruction. When you thought you made enough money, you tried to leave that life. The devil came in and took Precious from you. Am I right?"

"Yes you are right Cheri."

"You don't have to worry about me knowing about what happened in Florida. You and my daughter secrets are safe with me, but like I was saying you had to bring more death to get her back. Look what happened when Toya tried to walk away! She came back and lost her life. You tried to right the wrong of her death and during that time all mayhem broke loose. Sonya and Neicey lost theirs and Precious lands a life in prison. She was only 15 or 16 at the time and that was it for you. You wouldn't go back to hustling so the evil of the world threatened to take your son's mother again. You gave in to the hustle and now you are on a level that has your wife, my daughter afraid to live in a home that you were known to live in."

She let go of my hands and looked me dead in the eyes, "The devil has his favorite soldier back. I don't know what all you've done or to how many people, but Robert as you grow illegally in that lifestyle, the repercussions are going to be even greater."

"So was I supposed to sacrifice my family and sit idle and do nothing as I watch on?"

"No! When was the last time you prayed and let God?"

"Cheri I don't mean any disrespect but I do truly believe in God. I believe that God has made me for something, and right now he made me to save Lisa. He knows what I'm capable of doing and what I'm willing to do when situations occur. I believe he knows which route I will take before I do."

"Son listen to me. Do you really think God wants you to use your skills and personality to sell drugs and kill people?"

"Honestly I don't know what God wants with me!"

"Are you familiar with the Book of Job?"

"Vaguely."

"Then you know that the devil tempted Job and took everything he had and everyone he loved, but he didn't waiver. He stayed loyal to the Lord's word."

"Maybe God is letting me be drawn in, in order to kill the devil himself, or herself."

"I doubt it, remember thou shall not kill and vengeance is mine said the Lord."

"Yea but Moses killed that man for messing over that slave, and once he was on the run God came to him in the form of a burning bush. King David was a killer from the beginning and Paul was a killer of those who followed Christ when his name was Saul."

"Robert I don't know what God's plan with you is, but I know there has to be one, because of the high temptations that come your way. When things get rough pray on it and before you act out ask him to lead you."

"I believe a lot of what you just told me, but as you said every time I walk away I lose things and those I love. Right now I'm not trying to lose the lives of those I love. If I have to sacrifice my life and maybe even my soul in order for my family to be safe I'll do just that. Cheri, if I see the devil I'll be sure to cut his head off so I won't be tempted anymore."

I spent the rest of the night with my baby girls until they fell to sleep. Shree walked me to the door. "Your mom is deep. She really put some things on my mind."

"Yeah that's my mommy. She see's things others don't."

"Yea I guess she does." There was a moment of awkward silence. "Shree what's up with us?" She thought for a moment. "Robert I can't. I loved Ed, at least I thought I did and he's gone. I know I love you and I wanted nothing more than to have your baby and now that I have her, I have to make sure that I'll be around later in life. I can't follow you down this road any longer."

"I can respect that." I kissed her on the lips but she pulled back. "I can't."

"I understand." I turned to walk away. "Robert!"

"Yeah?"

"Please understand that I'll always be your wife and I'm here if you ever need me." I nodded my head and left.

Chapter 41 Lil Cuz

The girls were sitting in the living room watching Love & Hip-Hop Atlanta while I was getting dressed and packing my bag for a weekend long date. I came walking through the living room on my way out the door. Katrina openly displayed her dislike about me going out on dates, especially weekend long ones with women I'd met off the Internet. She rolled her eyes and smacked her lips loudly while sitting with her arms folded across her breast. "Ya'll gone be cool?" Kayla let it be known that they would be straight. Katrina mumbled with an attitude, "Un-uh."

"Alright I'll see ya'll Sunday night or Monday morning." Katrina couldn't hold back her dislike. "Yeah. Whatever! I don't understand you nigga. You got pussy right here. Two bad bitches might I add. I don't know why you been on those websites looking for sugar mama's like you need the money! I wish we would have never mentioned that part of our life to you."

"Man what's up with you?" She smacked her lips again.

"I thought so." She jumped up off the couch. "Thought so what!'

"What the fuck is wrong with you?"

"I'll tell you. I'm tired of you trying to act like a street nigga when you don't even need to. It's not cute and you don't need no money from no sugar mamas."

"I ain't trying to hear that. You mad because you think I'm doing something with her. She just wants company." Kayla just watched on. "Whateva! Why the fuck do she want to pay for dates for anyway? She's fine as hell, plus young. The bitch is like 25 or 26 and she wants to be with you for the whole weekend out in Miami and she's not trying to fuck? She don't even gotta pay for no dick or date! You need to cancel it!"

"You jealous that she's fine and young? You didn't have a problem with none of the old ugly ones!"

"You're stupid! I don't trust the bitch. Why are any of us still going on dates? Your dad said he's got us. We don't have any worries. He gave you this house. So please tell me why you are going on this date, or any others?"

"Because I'm my own man, I'm going to make my own money and if you don't like what I'm doing then leave. Remember you pulled me into this.

"Leave! You want me to leave?"

"Naw, but if you're going to keep bitching then bounce!"

Looking back at Kayla she threatened me. "If I go, we both go!" I looked at Kayla and she didn't make eye contact with me. "When I get back from Florida, you will still be here hopefully. If not then it's been fun." I walked out the door.

Chapter 42 Maria

Sitting at the vanity table in my bedroom wearing sexy lingerie, rubbing peach flavored body oil on I was looking forward to my plans tonight. "Jackie standing there looking upset mami isn't going to change anything. This is the right time, and he's the one I've chosen." She moved closer to me standing next to the mirror, "If that's what it's all about, why not have a doctor do it?" I didn't bother to look up at her. "Are we going to spend the rest of our lives dealing with you being jealous of me wanting a man from time to time?" She stared me down until I looked back at her. "What!!?"

"What? Are you fucking kidding me? This isn't what we agreed to. You said that we were going to use him to make Aza fall in love with him so we could use her plane. Now that the Cartel see's how much product we can move, we no longer need Aza's plane; but you seem to keep coming up with excuses to keep this asshole around."

"You really hate Cuz don't you?" Rolling her eyes and taking a death breath, "I wouldn't say hate but you know I can't stand him. He's fucking my woman. He also comes and goes from our home like he owns it. To make matters worse he really thinks he runs our drug empire. So yes! I do hate him!"

Standing face to face with Jackie I kissed her softly on her lips.

"He's not going to be around much longer!"

"You keep saying that, but he's still here!"

"Quit being like that. Baby you don't have anything to worry about. You won't lose me, not to Cuz or anyone." She walked away from me and flopped down on the bed. "Let me try to understand things. First he was just supposed to be our ticket to Aza's plane. You then allowed him to meet Hector. You know Hector is a male chauvinist pig! He has more male pride than he does Cuban pride so don't think for a second that he doesn't think our new expansion in the drug trade is because of Cuz. He's waging wars across the U.S. and bringing a lot of attention on himself. We don't want that attention on us Maria."

"I know he's done just what I knew he would." I flopped on the bed next to her. Jackie sat up quickly. "You planned on him doing this, and stealing your empire?"

Rolling over and kissing Jackie, "Always remember behind every great man there's an even colder bitch." Jackie began kissing me on the neck then reached between my legs. I was so hot but I had to stop her. I pulled away from her. "What the fuck Mimi!"

"You already know I'm ovulating. I don't want to waste my juices. I'm trying to make a little king that will take over everything I worked so hard for."

"You have never refused me since we been together."

"Calm down, anyway you have a date this weekend. Make the best of it."

"Ahhhh!!! The things I do for you. Maria this shit better be worth it. When it's time for Cuz to die, I want to do it."

"I might just let you. Now get up out of here before you miss your boy toy. Cuz will be here any minute."

Chapter 43 Cuz

Lying naked in the bed, sweating after an hour sex session with Maria I stared up at the ceiling. Maria was laying naked and worn out across my chest. "Papi what's on your mind?" I broke out of my ceiling stare trance. "I was just thinking." She rubbed her hands across my chest. "About round three?"

"Naw, but if you keep rubbing on me like that I'll mess around and put you to sleep!"

"Promises, promises, but seriously what are we going to with Aza now that Hector makes a way for us to get the product?"

"I don't understand. What you mean by, what we gone do with her?"

"If you decide to keep fucking her, how do you think she's going to react when the ceiling comes falling down?"

"You introduced her to me, now you sound like you want her dead or something."

She hit me on my chest. "Quit being stupid! I wouldn't dare bring that much heat on us. She's a real princess."

"So what the fuck are you talking about?"

"Cut her loose. You're too involved in our business. If something was to happen while she's around it'll be all over the news. Her people are keeping her over there because they've heard about you."

"Fuck them."

"No, no, no! Listen to me! You don't want those types of problems. Even I don't."

"Now you spooked? After you hooked me up with her to move your dope and as soon as you're able to get your shit without her, you want me to cut her off??"

"Have you fallen for her?"

"Not like that but she's good people. I see her as another way to come up."

Maria jumped on top of me. "Enough about her. You ready for round 3?"

"What's gotten into you?"

"Nothing can a girl enjoy sex with her man without something being up?"

"Oh so I'm your man now?"

"You know what I mean."

"No actually I don't so tell me."

"How about I show you?" She grabbed my dick and took me into her mouth. As soon as I was good and hard she stopped.

"What up?" She pulled me on top of her. "Round 3 is what's up."

"What's up with this missionary style shit?"

"It's my favorite." Thirty minutes in I began picking up my pace just as I was about to bust a nut; she wrapped her legs around me, grabbed me around my neck, and screamed out, "Cum in me!" I looked at her with confusion, she was acting weird. "Cum in me, I want to feel you nut in me!" I thought she was challenging me so I stroked harder and longer. "Oooh shit, oo-oooooh oh cu-cu-cum in me!"

She usually couldn't take the dick like this and begs me to stop by now. She had my ego kind of fucked up so I started power drilling her. "Yes! Ohhhh-myyyy-God you fucking me!" She went from wet to dry to wet again. I felt myself about to cum and tried to pull out. She grabbed me tighter to where I couldn't move and I released my seed inside of her and fell on top of her. I tried to roll off and up out of her. "No Papi leave it in."

"Girl if I didn't know any better I would think that you trying to get pregnant."

"I don't have time for kids, plus I'm on birth control. I won't have to worry about that for the next five years."

The next day Maria left me in her mansion while she went to her downtown office to take care of some business. I called a meeting with Ray-Ray, Jesse, and James who got there that afternoon. Ray-Ray had taken over distribution in the

Midwest, James had the East Coast, and Jesse the South. Sitting out on Maria's pool deck we began our meeting. "How's everything going in your areas?" Ray-Ray was the first to speak up, "Everything gravy my way, but you already knew that."

"I can't complain either since I'm plugged with the Bloods out of New York, they moving shit and laying niggas down that get in their way." James said. "The South straight. I'm just getting a little resistance in the A from them M.O.E niggas but once I know Big Moe's head off, everything will fall in line." Jesse said rubbing his chin.

"Just find out where he be at and get a picture of him. Send it to this P.O. Box."

"Cuz I can handle this nigga. He's just one muthafucka. I'll get him as soon as he shows his face."

"Jesse I'm not saying it like you can't take care of your biz but we kings now. We don't get our hands dirty unless we have to. You said the nigga went underground?"

"Yea his bitch ass hiding cause he knows I'm on his trail."

"Give him a week then shoot his OG in the ass, just enough to put her in the hospital." Jesse started laughing. "Cuz I ain't shooting his moms." I looked at him seriously until he stopped smiling. "Why not?"

"Cause she ain't got shit to do with what we doing in the streets."

"Remember this all of ya'll! Ain't no rules in these streets. We do what other niggas won't do. We on a whole different playing field than them other niggas. We not only in the NBA but we're on the All Star Team. Now if this is too much for ya'll let me know. I can put someone else in ya'll spots." They nodded their heads. "Alright Cuz don't trip. That old bitch will be in the E.R within the week."

"Good! I'm going to Cuba in the morning. My man over there wants to have a sit down with me. I got a feeling what it's about. By the way a certain person is acting, positions are threatened, so be leery of those that I put ya'll over. By that I mean, those that were already running their cities and doing their thang with ole girl before we came along."

Jesse was always the hot headed one. "I don't like watching my back amongst certain people. I'd rather kill them now."

"I respect that, but Jesse, you and James are now over the territories that were already in play with her. True enough we expanded that shit and organized it but I think that if they don't kill me in Cuba, then they are more or less going to give me the go ahead to outright take over Maria's shit full force. But we have to be careful, even though she's a woman; she's very dangerous and smart. I believe she knows that the Cartel don't want her anymore. She's smart enough to kill me and re-take over the operation after she kills ya'll. So like I said before, be watchful of the people she had in play."

"That's why I say we kill them niggas now and the bitch too!" I looked around to see if we were still alone. "Calm down Jess, I'm just thinking ahead. If the Cubans don't want her touched then she's not to be touched. As far as the people that Maria has in place, go ahead, but only after you find others to replace them. Then it won't slow down our operation. Don't let it be known that we had it done."

We all stood up as our way of saying meeting over. "Alright Cuz. I'll get with ya'll. I'm a head back to my hotel. I got a bad little bitch I brought down here with me." Ray-ray said with the biggest grin I'd seen all day. "Jess, James, if ya'll need my help with anything just give me a holla. I got some killers up my way that's begging for some work."

"Good looking out. I'm straight tho. My East Coast niggas love putting that work in."

"And ya'll know I love this type of shit. Money and murder is what I live for." Jesse said.

Chapter 44 Precious

China has been gone for about five months now and Missy a little bit after her. Tammy has less than four months left and with the new crack law, Rosa has less than two years to do. Everyone that I've grown to know and love all seems to leave. I don't want my friends to spend the rest of their lives in prison, but seeing everyone leaving like they do, makes having a life sentence that much harder. I had Mrs. Roche to deal with Rosa for the k-2 and tobacco. I didn't feel like being bothered with it and it's not like I needed the money.

Last month my lawyer told me that he had oral arguments in the 7th Circuit Court of Appeals. He believes that my case has a strong chance of winning. That hope is just about the only thing that keeps me going. If it wasn't for that hope I'd break and lose my mind. All I've been doing lately is hanging in my cell, using my phone to talk to China and Cuz, and praying. Praying is something that I've never done before. I'm learning about faith and it's helping my get through this. .China told me that Cuz as fucking with the bitch name Maria tough. I always knew that bitch had her eye on him back when her brother was alive.

Tammy and Rosa came by my cell to see if I was going if I was going to chow. I had stopped eating out the chow hall months ago. Every now and then I'd go on Thursdays if they had fried chicken. "Baby girl I know you ain't on some depressed shit again in this cell. Come on out this cell girl. It ain't going no where."

"Very funny Rosa, but for real ya'll I'm cool. I'm just taking some time out to get my thoughts together. Ya'll know if I come out all these bitches gone come running to me with their problems."

"Fuck them hoes. That's what you got me and Felicia for."

"Rosa I know you and Felicia be standing on everybody. Ya'll won't give anybody a break. I just need some me time."

"Rosa I know what she's saying. Let's give her some time." Tammy said grabbing Rosa by the arm. "Alright Baby girl see ya later."

"Alright ya'll. Come back and holla at me after chow."

When they left I began getting myself together. I figured I'd go outside for an hour. I was standing at my sink brushing my teeth when Rosa came back. "I know damn well ya'll ain't made it to chow hall that fast."

"Ok mami! You got jokes. No I came back to tell you Mrs. Roche wants to see you in her office."

"Alright! If it ain't one thing, it's another."

"What you think she wants?"

"Ain't no telling, after I finish brushing my teeth I'll go back there."

"See you when you get back."

I went to the back the unit and knocked on the door where my counselor's office was. The secretary Mrs. Thompkins let me in. Mrs. Roche waved me into her office. "Close the door behind you." She was on the phone with a serious look on her face. "Yes, she's sitting right here now, okay thanks." She hung up the phone, smiling at me. "What's going on?"

"I have some great news for you."

"If it ain't about getting out of here then it can't be great."

"Well Precious, I guess it's great new because you've been ordered released immediately."

I began shaking, "Mrs. Roche don't play with me on the real." She smiled. "Oh, no! I'm not playing at all. I just got off the phone with the warden. All charges have been dismissed by the appeals court, and for the record, how old are you really?"

"20, why?"

"That's one of the reasons. You were a juvenile at the time of the offense. You have over twenty thousand dollars on your account. We'll supply you with a bus ticket to wherever you want to go, or I can purchase you a plan ticket from the funds off your inmate account. Which will it be?"

I began crying. I was overwhelmed. "You serious? You not bull-shitting? I can go home? I can really go home?" She got up and walked around her desk and gave me a hug. "Yes. I'm very serious. Precious you are not a bad person. Life just happened to you. Make your release count." Still crying I managed to continue talking, "I will. Can I make a phone call?"

"Sure, here use my phone." I dialed Cuz's cell and it went straight to voicemail. "Damn it!" I then dialed China.

"Hello?"

"Aye, guess what?

"Baby girl?"

"Yesssss, I'm getting out today! Can you believe it?"

"Don't fuckin play with me! You coming home to me?

"Yes." China began to scream with joy. "Hey calm down. I need a ride to come pick me up. I tried to call Daddy but no answer."

"He has a condo right in Miami. I got keys. I'll call car service to pick you up and take you to a hotel til I get there. I'm hopping on the next flight."

"Okay don't tell Cuz that I'm getting out. I want to surprise him."

"Okay love you! See you in a little bit."

"Love you too! Okay bye."

"Well go pack up your things you want to keep. The sooner you're ready, the sooner we can get you out of here! Congratulations Precious!"

"Thank you, thank you so much! Don't worry I'll be done packing before you know it! You don't have to tell me twice. I'm outta here!"

I came speed walking from Mrs. Roche office just as Rosa and Tammy were coming back into the unit. Rosa noticed my pace. "Why you in such a rush? You got a date or something?" I waved them into my cell. I was frantically moving through my things. I was collecting all my pictures, letters, and legal papers. Tammy was looking at me like I was crazy. "Baby girl what ya doing? Moving?" I just nodded my head. "Where to?"

"Yeah where to? Rosa said. I couldn't hold it any longer. "I'm getting the hell out of here!!" I hugged both them!! "Wait, wait! Baby girl are you alright?" Rosa said as she put her hand on my forehead like she was checking if I had a fever.

I stopped and looked my best friend in her eyes, with my hands on my hips. "Yes Rosa! I'm fine! They dismissed all my charges. I was only 15 when that shit happened." We all screamed and started jumping around. They helped me pack up the rest of my things before we said our goodbyes. "Ya'll can split the rest of this shit up. Rosa you can keep the cell phone. I'm gone!"

"I'm so happy for you. You didn't deserve to be here for life."

"Thank you Tammy. I'll see you when you get out and Rosa I'll see soon also. You gone get that time off for that new crack law. I just know it."

She started tearing up. "Just promise to throw me the biggest party ever."

"You know I got you!" They walked me to R&D and two hours later there was a black limo waiting to pick me up.

Chapter 45 Maria

I was sitting in my office with Titio the head of my security team looking at the computer screen. I was watching Cuz talk about killing off the men that were down with me from the beginning. "Titio I want you to make sure his men never leave Miami alive."

"I'm on it! What about Cuz?"

"Leave him to me! I'll deal with him when he gets back from Cuba myself. I picked up the phone and called Jackie. "Hello!"

"It's time to move baby! Time to teach Mr. Cuz who the baddest bitch from Cuba is."

"I've been waiting for this day mami!!!!! This I will enjoy probably a little bit more than tasting your sweet juices."

"Do you have everything in place?"

"Of course. My part has been taken care of."

"Well get ready for a few more to join your party!"

"I will show no mercy!"

"That's my baby!" I knew Jackie would do her job and do it well. I sat back smiling at the unexpected twist that Cuz would not be ready for. I knew that like any other man, pussy would be his down fall. It just took the right pussy, mine! He thought he was so different from other men. I was about to show him differently; show him that pussy was the root of all evil and not money. He was finally about to meet his match. I got up and walked to the mirror in my office and admired myself in all my glory. "I bet Cuz will wish he would've watched more carefully who he lays with because this time he laid with the devil."

Chapter 46 James

My brother and I decided to step out to Club Underground, a strip club. We loved this place because they never searched us; plus they allowed us to engage in all the extra sexual activities we wanted. The club was dark and the lights were dim except for the three stages. Club Underground had a different erotic feel from your ordinary strips clubs. You could swim in the pool with strippers, shower, or even catch an oil wrestling fight all for the right price. It was so hot in there that even at 2 p.m. in the afternoon it would be jumping with a line around the corner at night like your local nightclubs.

When we entered we were instantly given a V.I.P. booth and a free bottle of Ace of Spades. The owner Teya, who was an exotic mix of Cuban and Jamaican, came to greet us at our table wearing skin tight black spandex leggings with a sheer black lace strapless crop top. "Hello gentlemen how are my two favorite men doing?" I looked at Jesse because he had a serious thing for Teya. "Shit we gravy now that you're here, but I'd be better if you sat and had a drink with me." I laughed and shook my head. I knew he never had a chance with Teya; plus he had already fucked just about every stripper in Club Underground.

Teya proved me wrong when she sat down in the booth with us and nudged me on my knee to scoot over so she can sit between us. As she made her way between us she brushed her ass up against Jesse and then sneakily rubbed on my dick. "A girl could use a good stiff drink, and a couple stiff----let me quit before you guys lose respect for me." She grabbed both us high on our thighs, and we both looked at each other. A topless thong wearing waitress appeared with a gold bottle trimmed in black diamonds and three shot glasses.

"Ace of Spaces isn't my drink of choice. I'm more of a Louis the 13 and Hen XO kind of girl; especially when I'm going to fuck two brothers."
"That what I'm talking about." Jesse yelled. The waitress poured the three shots and handed them to us. We held our drink up to toast. Teya said, "To us!" We clicked our glasses and downed our drink; before I knew it everything faded to black.

Chapter 47 Ray-Ray

I was drying off after my shower getting ready to take my new girl Neitra site seeing in Miami. "Ray I would really love to spend the rest of my life down here. The people that live here are so lucky." I started putting on my wife beater and cargo shorts, "Yeah it is beautiful ain't it?"

"I've been out on the balcony all morning looking at the ocean and the yachts."

"I might take you out on one of those big boats before we leave."

"Okay!" There was a knock at the door. "Ray you expecting anyone?"

"Naw! Did you order room service?"

"Uh-uh." I looked out the peep hole. "Well that's who it is."

"Well open the door then!" I opened the door. "Yeah?"

"Complimentary brunch."

The Latin guy came through the door pushing a cart of delicious looking food. "Would you like me to set your meal up on the balcony?" Neitra was all smiles and looking at me like I was the sweetest man on earth. "I didn't order." Neitra cut me off. "Ray this is so nice." She looked at his name tag. "Jose you can set it up on the balcony." She pulled me by my arm and put it around her as she hugged me tightly around my waist.

Once he set the table, we sat as he served us our food.

"Would you like vodka in your juice?"

"Naw man! It's too early for that shit."

"It's the best in the house."

"Yes pour us a shot in our juices, come on Ray we're on vacation."

"Alright! What the lady wants. The lady gets!"

Chapter 48 Cuz

When I boarded the private jet to Cuba I turned my phone off to avoid any distractions. I had to have my thoughts together because this meeting would determine my life as far as if I lived or died. A lot of what Shree's mom said had stuck with me and it was heavy on my mind. The leer landed on the private air strip where it was met by military personnel. I was escorted to a Hummer and driven to a wooded area that was turned into a shooting range. Hector was at the range shooting a fifty caliber assault rifle. He turned from looking down the barrel of his rifle when he saw us approaching.

I stood next to him as he returned focused back to his target. "You know why I sent for you?"
"I have a few ideas." He nodded towards a pair of binoculars. I picked them up and looked towards his target. His men were over two-hundred yards away tying a woman to a post. "She worked in my kitchen. She was caught stealing food for her family." We both made eye contact with each other. He looked away, took aim, and shot her in the chest. "If I would have missed she could have lived." I didn't like the situation, but it wasn't any concern of mine. He offered me a cigar, which I accepted even though I didn't smoke.

When people like Hector offer you something, you accept or he feels offended. One of his men lit his cigar then mine. We walked back to the Hummer and he opened the door for me. "Sometimes a bitch has to be taken out back and put out like a dog. Especially if she out grows her worth. There won't be any new shipments until I only deal with one person in the states." He walked away from me. I climbed in the Hummer and was driven back to the plane.

Once I was out of Cuban airspace I tried to call my guys. Neither of them answered. When I ended my last call my phone rang a Miami number. I assumed it was Ray-Ray since I knew he was chilling there for a while. "Ray-Ray!"
"No Daddy, it's me Precious! I got out today." I felt like I was dreaming. "Baby girl?"
"Huh?"
"It's you for real?" She started laughing, "Yeah, where you at?"
"I'm on my way back. I'm going to send my bodyguards to come get you and bring you to me. Where you at?"
"I'm at The Hilton downtown. Room 224."
"Anybody know you out?"
"China! She's on her way down here."

"Call her back and tell her wait for Lisa and to meet us at the airport in Indianapolis. I don't know what time we will be there but tell her to be ready. She'll know what I mean."

"Why are you sounding nervous instead of happy? Is everything okay?"

"I don't know, but don't let nobody in your room. Wait for Big Tree to come get you. He's going to bring you to me."

"Alright."

"I'm calling Tree now. I'll see you soon. I love you Baby girl."

"Love you too Daddy."

After I hung up with Precious I tried calling Ray-Ray, Jesse, and James again and still wasn't getting an answer.

"Man this bitch Maria moves fast!" I called Lisa. "Hello!"

"Aye Lisa it's that time. Get with Lil Rob and ya'll get with my mother and head out to China's place."

"Already Robert?"

"Look I don't have time for this. It's on, so please move. I got to make some calls." I hung with her and called China and my security team. It was on.

Chapter 49 Lil Cuz

I woke up gagged and tied down to a chair in what looked like a cabin or a small house. The last thing I remembered was riding with Lady J my date, and drinking some strong liquor. Not only do I not know where I'm at, but I don't know how long I've been here. I was beginning to panic then I heard a few people talking as they began coming down the stairs. Five big muscle built looking dudes came down carrying three other niggas that were handcuffed and knocked out.

I had never seen nothing like this before and I damn near shitted on myself. They proceeded to chain the three guys up by their wrists to shackles that were hanging from the ceiling. There were two more sets of shackles left and I prayed one wasn't for me. Once they had the men hanging by their wrists, they looked at me. The biggest of them said, "Look the little punk is woke." I damn near stopped breathing. I began to wonder what happened to Lady J. No sooner than I thought about her she came walking down the steps. I was relieved to see her but then the way she mugged me let me know she was in on it.

I tried to give her my most pleading look possible. She took charge. "Wake them up!" The big guys began slapping the three guys until they woke up. Lady J walked over to the steel table and opened up a case of big shiny steel knives and saws. She walked up to one of the guys with what looked to be a machete in her hand. The guy she walked up to looked around the room, then back to her. "Who the fuck are you?"

"The last bitch you'll ever see!" Then he spoke to other guys. "So this is how we go out huh James and Ray-Ray?"

"Yea Bro! It was real. I had a ball."

"Me too, but one thing ya'll got to know for sure Jesse and James is Cuz is going to go hard for us. We lived as gangsters, so let's die like gangsters." I then realized these were my dad's men.

"Isn't that sweet, but I promise you'll scream like bitches!" She swung the machete and sliced the guy across his chest opening him up. He screamed out louder than I've ever heard a man scream. The other man hanging next to him screamed too. "Bitch that's my little brother! I'm a kill you!" She walked in front of him and he tried to kick at her, when he missed, he spit on her. She sliced him across his chest. "Cuz ain't going to do shit but die like you." I actually shitted on myself for real. The big guy close to me covered his nose. "Awe man this little bitch shit his pants." Lady J turned and

221

looked at me. "Lil Cuz, one thing for sure you're nothing like your father." They all began laughing. The third guy began staring at me then spoke up. "What is it that ya'll want?" One of the men socked him in the face. "We didn't ask you to speak."

Lady J walked over to me and wiped the blood off the blade with my shirt. "Lil Cuz, you shouldn't have never been so easy to get. You go against your father's word so much that it was piece of cake to bait you; but now I bet you wish you would have done everything he ever told you. I'm going to change your life forever. You're going to watch me chop your father's men up into pieces and if I get the word you're next." The last guy hanging that hadn't been cut yet yelled, "Leave him out of this bitch. You're signing your own death certificate." She turned to her men, "Shut him up!" They made me watch as they chopped and sawed the three guys into pieces.

Chapter 50 Cuz

When I landed in Miami, Big Tree and six of my best men were waiting for me. The door to the SUV opened and Big Tree and my men got out leading a short, thick, gray sweat suit wearing female on to the jet. I was overjoyed just seeing her. She was beyond fine, this girl, I mean woman has always had my heart and now she was mature enough for me to completely give it to her. She sat on my lap and kissed me. "Hey Daddy." I smiled, but it quickly faded away. "What's up Baby girl?" "You!" She reached in for another kiss. I held her up because the call I was waiting for came through. "Aza? Precious looked at me upset. I looked at her and shook my head. "Remember that emergency favor I told you that I might need one day?"

"Yes."

"Well I need it asap."

"Ok, um okay. Where do you want me to meet them?"

"Indianapolis Airport. I'll have their passports and everything ready."

"I'll pick them up tomorrow. That's the earliest I can make it. I'll call you with a time."

"Okay thanks, and Aza?"

"Yes?"

"Thanks baby. This means the world to me."

"Don't worry but baby I can't bring them here. How about I take them to my place in France? They'll bend in better there."

"If you think it will be best. I trust you, and sweetheart I'm trusting you with my whole life with this one."

"Anything for my prince, you just make it out safe."

"I will."

Precious got off my lap. "That was your Arab chic?"

"Yeah. She's from Kuwait. She's good people. You'll get to meet her soon because you're going to France with her and my family."

"Why? What's going on?" The plane was refueled and we took off for Indianapolis. I told Precious everything that had been going on since she's been gone. "Daddy I'm not going to France while you're out here fighting that bitch. If she got Ray-Ray, Jesse, and James then you are going to need all the help you can get. If anything happens to you or me, it's going to happen to both of us together. I'm not losing you again. I just got you back."

We landed in Indianapolis and were met by the rest of my security team. They drove us to China's place and when we got there Lisa and my mother were looking worried. Lisa ran up to me, "I can't find him."

"Who?"

"Rob, I can't find Lil Rob."

"You called his phone?"

"Yes nigga of course I did!"

"Calm down! I'll call his girlfriend." When I called the house his girl Katrina answered and told me everything about how they were taking date on some website called Sugarbabies.com and how Lil Rob went to Miami with an attractive Hispanic woman that looked to be in her twenties. "Katrina do you know what she looks like?"

"Yes I can actually send you a picture of her from the computer."

"Do that asap."

My heart dropped. It sounded like she was describing Jackie's evil ass. When the picture came through to my phone, my worse nightmare had come true. It was Jackie. I had to sit down. "What's wrong? Where's my baby?" All I could do was shake my head. Lisa attacked me. I had to hold her down then her youngest son started crying. "Lisa calm down. Mama take Lil Kris upstairs to one of the bedrooms." My mother had tears in her eyes but she led him upstairs. Lisa was crying harder. "Is my son dead?"

"Naw I don't think so. I got to make a call but I have to do it in private."

"No I want to talk to whoever has my son!!!" I grabbed her by her shoulders and made her look at me. "I need you to hold it together. I'm going to do everything I possibly can to bring our son home. Okay?" She just nodded her head. "Go upstairs and comfort Lil Kris so he can stop worrying."

I called Maria. "Hello?" I chose my words and my tone wisely. "I guess the best way to go about this is to cut the bullshit."

"Okay, what can I do for you?"

"I want my son."

"I don't know what you're talking about." I was getting upset.

"Don't play with me. I know he's with Jackie. I want him back now!"

"Robert you're not running shit sweetheart, so don't ever give me an order." There was silence. "Now what can I do for you?"

"I want my son Maria, so let him go."

"Why should I? You want him back? Turn yourself over to my people and I'll let him go."

"How I know he's still alive?"

"You don't but you don't have a choice."

"Now you're playing games with the wrong nigga. Bitch you'll be dead before the sun rises tomorrow!"

She bellowed out the most evil laugh I had ever heard. "I love when you talk dirty to me. You make me so horny. Robert we could have made a hell of a team."

"Maria give me back my son!" She hung up on me. I tried to call back but I was sent straight to voicemail. I gave up after an hour.

I made arrangements for my best, go hard killers to meet me at the one of my stash houses. I had to pull out all the stops so I had to hit up Brahead and The Alley boys as well. They were monsters with the gunplay and running Chiraq. I never stepped on their toes and vice versa. I needed them all the enforcement I could get right now. When I reached out, Brahead was in with no questions asked. "Man, Brahead I owe you big time for this."

"Man Joe, whatever you need. We ready. Me and my niggas on the next flight to Miami. I'll hit you when we make it."

"We about to bring war to Miami. This evil ass bitch took my only son, so now I have to crush the bitch's whole empire."

"Let's get it done."

I had to hold a house meeting that night. I waited for Shree, here mother, and my daughters to arrive. Once everyone was there and the kids were all sleeping, I gathered them all into the living room. "Tomorrow evening around 5 o'clock a friend of mine is going to meet ya'll at the airport and fly ya'll to France. You all knew that one day this day might come and it's here. Unfortunately Lil Rob has gotten himself caught up in this shit." Lisa began crying out loud. My mother hugged her as they both cried and I continued to talk.

"I'm a do everything in my power to bring him back, even if it means trading him for me. These people are so evil. They might have already killed him. They may be using the thought of getting him back as a weakness against me." I looked at them to make sure they were understood and was getting what I was saying. "I've set up offshore accounts for my exit plan. My friend Aza is going to show ya'll how to blend in over there in France and set ya'll up with a comfortable place to live."

Precious jumped in, "I ain't going nowhere without you! I already told you that. Why you sounding like you ain't coming back?"
"Precious this shit I done got myself in is truly life or death. I lost Sonya, Neicey, and Toya to this game. I can't sacrifice the lives of those I love anymore." I began choking up. "I-I may have lost my son." My mother stopped me, "Stop saying that. There is power in the tongue. You're going to bring my

grandson home. Now do what you got to do but promise that you coming back with my grandson."

I knew I couldn't promise that. I knew what I was dealing with. "I promise I'll do everything in my power and if God's willing I'll bring Lil Rob home." Precious walked me to the door. "Daddy take me with you. How you know them niggas got your back?" I wrapped my arms around her and cuffed her ass. "Baby girl, I can't have your blood on my hands; plus if I don't make it I'll happily rest in peace knowing you're safe."

"As long as I'm with you I'm safe no matter what's going on." "I believe you. It's just that I need someone I can trust and depend on to watch over my family. Baby girl even though you're the youngest I know you are the strongest and the smartest. You're a leader and I need you to protect my home." She hook her head, "If you want me to make sure your family is straight then that's what I'll do but understand I'd rather be fighting right by your side." I kissed her, "I know Baby girl. I love you." I left out the door, climbed into the S.U.V and headed out.

Chapter 51 Maria

I turned on my cell phone that Cuz had the number to. "Eighty missed calls."

"I see your super stud isn't so hard to scare as you thought he was Mimi." I didn't answer Jackie. I decided to listen to some of his begging messages. The first ten or so he was begging for me to return his son unharmed. Then he began begging to just hear his voice. The last message shook me. "Maria I'm done calling. You want to play big then it's on! My son is already dead to me. I'm going to destroy everything and everybody around you. Your name won't be worth shit to anyone by the time this is over."

Jackie and Titio laughed. "Can you believe the balls on this nigger? Mocking his voice, "My son is already dead to me."

"Titio! This isn't a joke. We're dealing with a man who has given up hope."

"Fuck that black son of a bitch! Me and my men will find him and kill him!"

"Titio stop acting like a man! He's trying to call us out into the open for a fight, remember he has snipers and people specializing in explosives."

"Baby why you sound like you're afraid of him?"

"Jackie I'm not afraid of him. You have to know and understand your enemy in order to beat them. I was banking on him turning himself over to us in exchange for his son. I think I over played my hand by not answering his calls."

"We can still let him talk to the little pussy."

"Titio go out to the Everglades, clean him up, feed him, and bring him here."

"What? I thought we were going to kill him and his little bastard and feed them to the gators?"

"Do as I say and do it now!" When Titio walked away the phone rang. "Hello?" It was one of business partners. "You're kidding me! When and why am I just hearing of this? Have Melita talk to the investigators. Call me back when they're gone."

"What? What is it?" Jackie said frantically. "The downtown office and our high end boutique stores were burned down last night."

"They're insured, so what?"

"So what!!! Jackie those are my legit businesses. He's waging a public drug war with me. Everything I worked for, my reputation and all will be ruined because of this asshole!"

Chapter 52 Precious

The security detail led us to the airport with the kids. We were in the private plane area of the airport when a big gold colored airplane landed. A passenger van pulled up to take us to the plane. I wasn't feeling this shit not one bit. How in the world am I supposed to just get on a plane to France without knowing if Cuz is alive! I was getting nauseous just thinking of it. Mr. Smith met us at the plane and handed us our passports. Me and China's had false names.

When the door to the plane opened a bitch came out dressed in a green and gold I dream of Genie outfit. I couldn't believe it. This nigga done really pulled a rich Arab bitch. Edwina and LaNeice thought she was something special and everyone was being extra nice to her. I couldn't stand the sight of her. She tried to talk to me. "You must be Precious, the one he calls Baby girl?"

"Yeah!" She reached out to shake my hand. "I'm Aza. Robert told me to tell you that I'm more than happy to be one of your sisters." She was too rich and too pretty. I wasn't leaving the country with her, but I had to fake it.

I extended my hand back to her. "I'm glad to meet you too. He's told me so much about you." She smiled. "Oh really?"

"Yea he told me that you can be trusted, so here's the thing! Shree, Lisa, I'm not going. Take care of the kids and your mothers. China stay here with me. I can't leave like this."

"Precious what you doing?"

"Shree I'm going down there to find Cuz and help him. I just can't leave him like this, hell this passport is under a phony name for a reason. If I leave him I'll be as phony as the name on my passport."

"So what are you going to do?"

"I'm a get with my girls and the rest of the security team and go down there and get my man back!"

Mr. Smith butted in. "Ms. Jones I don't think that's a good idea that you get involved. It's very serious!"

"Mr. Smith we're very serious! We started this with him from the beginning. Shree you remember Cuz and The Hustle Bunnies! We in it for the love our man and for the love of the hustle."

"Alright! Ma take Edwina and LaNeice to France. I'll see ya'll later."

"Shree you sure?"

"Yeah mama. He's my husband, til death do us part."

Lisa stepped up. "Mrs. Wilson I'm going to go with them too. Take care of Lil Kris for me. I can't just sit back and wait to see if they gone bring my son back plus I'm to blame for most of this."

"Ya'll young women should leave this fighting and killing to my son. I know ya'll love him but you can lose your lives." I held Mrs. Wilson's hand. "Mrs. Wilson we all have lost our lives in one way or another. This is what life with your son is and we all knew it when we chose to be with him. Aza would you please take care of Cuz's babies, mother, and mother-in-law?"

"Yes Precious. He told me that you were a true leader and when I see you all again I'll throw you the biggest party in Dubi."

"We'll look forward to it."

Chapter 53 Cuz

I had been studying the escape tunnels that Maria had built into her mansion. I was hoping she didn't change the codes to the doorways that lead to a secluded part of the beach. Instead of escaping I was going to use her tunnels to invade. She had three ways to enter the tunnels from her mansion. One was in her home office, the other was through the wall of her walk-in closet, and another was in her basement work out center. They all had hidden key pads that I just happen to have the passwords to.

I knew she would hold up in her mansion because it was built like a fortress. She lived on the other side of Miami where all the super rich lived so that was also to her advantage. There was guarded security just to cross the bridge over into that area. That was their way of protecting their rich from the common folks. I knew once the shit hit the fan and the guns started blasting there would be only a few minutes before the whole police force showed up.

When night fell upon the city of Miami me and twelve of my best men were going into Maria's place on a mission of death. I stared at the escape tunnels and dropped to my knees in prayer. I knew the only way I could ever make it out of this alive was with God by my side. "Heavenly Father I come to you not as a soldier of the devil but as one of your soldiers. I know my choices are not as you see fit, but I know I'm your child and not one of his. I ask that you cover me on this mission. As you gave your life for us, I'll gladly give my life for my son and for the rest of my family to be safe. I ask that you go in before me. Forgive me for the murders that are about to occur. I'm prepared to be judged for it later. In Jesus name I pray amen."

I came from off my knees and gave my men the order to move. We made it into the tunnel a little after eleven at night. The first entrance we came across was the one to her workout center. I tried the code I had and the hidden door opened. My man Blu was leading the first team of four in through the basement. When he peeked a look inside her gym he was shot in the head, then more gunfire followed. We returned fire as we began backing back down through the tunnel.

Big Tree let off a barrage of shots with his street sweeper trying to give us time to flee back out the tunnel but midway to the exit we were met with more gun fire. We were trapped. Maria's voice came over the intercom system. "Cuz did you really think I showed you those tunnels because I trusted you? I showed them to you with the hope that you would use them." Her evil laugh echoed through the tunnels. I was thinking to myself what happened to the shy, quiet lady she appeared to be when Ricky was alive? A woman can damn sure put on many forms. "These tunnels are sound proof. You'll die there. I have over twenty-five heavily armed men ready to flush you out." She laughed again. "And your son can watch you die on the monitor, isn't that right?"

"Dad!!!"

"Little Rob! Fuck you bitch! Send them bitch ass niggas in. I got something for them!"

No sooner than I said that, the ground shook and the lights in the tunnel flickered off and on. You could hear Maria screaming over the speakers. "Titio get back up here. They're attacking the main gate!" Then the ground shook again.

Chapter 54 Precious

China snuck along the wall on the sides of Maria's home and placed bombs all around the mansion. After China blew open the two sides of the wall surrounding the house, along with eight men rushed through one hole; while Shree, Lisa, and ten more of the men in our security rushed the house from the other side. Missy had set up a sniper post on the highest point of the wall. There were only two armed guards at the front of the house and Missy took them out easily.

China laced the big front door with plastic explosives, we cleared the porch and she blew the double doors in. We headed up the big spiral staircase looking for Cuz. As both teams made it halfway up the stairs gun fire broke out behind us. A group of armed men came out of nowhere. We had a slight advantage being that we were elevated, but her men made it out into the foyer shooting at us. Five of them were shot down and three of our men were hit as well. We kept moving up the stairs.

It sounded like a whole new war had kicked off from where then men had come from. More of her men came running out from the back, but they weren't shooting at us.

They were firing in the direction from which they came. A couple of grenades went off and it cleared away all of Maria's men and gave us enough of a distraction to clear the stairs. We took cover on the upper deck as gun shots continued to bust off, then I heard him. "Yeah bitch! Let's kill each other!" Cuz, Big Tree, and Brahead came around the corner carrying big boy guns. "Daddy! It's me Precious!" I jumped out from the cover I was taking. Cuz and his men ran up the stairs and joined us. "Baby girl what are you doing here?"

"I told you I'm a live and die by your side."

"Me too!"

"Shree?"

"And me!"

"Lisa!! Man what the fuck are ya'll doing here?"

China answered, "To blow some shit up for you!"

Chapter 55 Cuz

I couldn't stay and talk to the girls. I took off running towards Maria's office. When I kicked the door in Maria stood behind her office chair with my son tied to it and a gun to this head. Jackie was standing to the side of her pointing two guns at us. "Don't take another step, or I'll blow his head off!" I stepped into her office followed by Precious, Lisa, Shree, and China. "I'm not fucking playing! Don't try me!" Lil Rob's eyes were swollen shut and he was beat up pretty bad. Lisa was horrified."What the fuck did you do to my baby?"

"Mom? Dad?" He began crying. Jackie looked down at him. "Shut the fuck up."

"Maria you know this place is going to be crawling with police and FEDs. I'm willing to call this off. We all can get up out of here before they show up."

"Shut the fuck up! You ruined everything I've built. My name is ruined in the legit circuit. Hector will never do business with me because of this!"

"You did this. We could have worked together."

"Really? You stupid son of a bitch my pool deck is monitored. I heard every word you said to those three dead assholes!"

Sirens could be heard in the distance. "We running out of time Maria. We all could use the tunnel and get out of here." She looked like she was considering the offer. "Don't be stupid Maria. He's still going to kill us once he has us in the tunnel. Let's take his son and if he follows us, we kill the boy." "Don't listen to her that'll be suicide. You're smarter than that." Glass broke from the window behind the desk and Jackie dropped with a new hole in her head. Maria ducked down away from the window but she still kept her gun fixed on Lil Rob.

"Cuz I'll take your offer, but I have to tell you something first!"

"What?"

"I'm pregnant. I'm having your baby!"

"Oh hell naw! What??" Precious yelled.

"Yeah right."

"It's the truth, so I know you won't kill me knowing I'm carrying your seed, so call off your sniper and I'll put down my gun."

"China call off Missy." She texted Missy and a few minutes later Missy was in the office with us.

Maria put down her gun and began opening the doorway to the tunnel. The sirens were louder and a chopper could be heard flying over the house. Lisa and Shree ran over and cut Lil Rob from the chair. "Okay ya'll let's get up out of here. We got like a five mile run ahead of us."

"Cuz I'll lead the way and show you to my other home with speedboats attached to the dock." We followed Maria through her underground maze. This route was new to me. It was in the opposite direction from which we came.

When we entered the other residence and saw that the getaway was true, my men loaded up the speedboats while my girls, my son, and Maria boarded her yacht. Precious pulled her nine millimeter on Maria. "This is the end of the road for you bitch!"

"I'm carrying his baby. You can't kill me! Cuz you gave me your word!"

"Yeah I did, but she didn't, plus we fucked less than a week ago! I wouldn't even call it an abortion."

"What??"

"Bye bitch!" Precious shot her twice in the head, and pushed her body into the water. We were rid of the devil that had been secretly controlling our lives for years.

A couple days later, I woke up in a super king size bed with Precious, China, Lisa, Shree, and Aza. Precious was lying across my chest. She woke up when I moved. "Good morning."

"Good morning, Baby girl."

"You got to be the luckiest man in the world."

"I know huh? Five must be my lucky number!" She laughed.

"So you think you can legally marry five women in France?"

Contact Information
Connect with Shaunta'e!

Instagram: @achocolatekiss

Twitter: @hustle_bunnies and @achocolatekiss

Facebook: www.facebook.com/AuthorShauntae

Website: www.brandnullc.com

Email: Hustlebunnies1@gmail.com

Made in the USA
Charleston, SC
15 February 2016